Praise for
How to Finish Everythi

"Unfinished tasks are truly an epidemic. I was inspired by reading Jan Yager's *How to Finish Everything You Start* and I also experienced deep introspection in doing the exercises."
—Ajeet Khurana, CEO

"Dr. Jan Yager's new book, *How to Finish Everything You Start*, zeros in on the real reasons why we often don't finish what we begin, and more importantly, what we can do to get over the obstacles that stand in our way."
—Don Gabor, author of *How to Start a Conversation and Make Friends*

"In this fast-paced, get-it-done environment, the real pressure is that to compete you must complete. Jan Yager draws on original research and her expertise in time management to help you identify the possible causes behind your failure to finish. She offers real-life examples, practical tips, and she poses thoughtful questions to help you enhance your performance and get the right things done. A great read from start to finish!"
—Linda Swindling, JD, CSP, author of *The Manager's High-Performance Handbook*

"Jan Yager's *How to Finish Everything You Start* is a must-read for anyone who is a go-getter out of the gate, but who often or just from time to time lacks the follow-through it takes to cross the finish line. In this straight-forward guide, Dr. Yager shares pragmatic and actionable advice which will move you to get things done. Read this book – and finish it – to learn from a prolific producer who truly understands the importance of, and the art of, completion."
—Wendi McNeill, Founder, Charli Jane Speakers

How to Finish Everything You Start

HABITS TO TRANSFORM YOUR LIFE

Jan Yager

JAICO PUBLISHING HOUSE

Ahmedabad Bangalore Chennai
Delhi Hyderabad Kolkata Mumbai

Published by Jaico Publishing House
A-2 Jash Chambers, 7-A Sir Phirozshah Mehta Road
Fort, Mumbai - 400 001
jaicopub@jaicobooks.com
www.jaicobooks.com

Published in arrangement with
Hannacroix Creek Books, Inc.
1127 High Ridge Road, #110
Stamford, CT 06905-1203 USA

To be sold only in India, Bangladesh, Bhutan,
Pakistan, Nepal, Sri Lanka and the Maldives.

HOW TO FINISH EVERYTHING YOU START
ISBN 978-93-87944-76-3

First Jaico Impression: 2019
Ninth Jaico Impression: 2023

Page design and layout: Bharati Composers, Delhi

Printed by
Trinity Academy For Corporate Training Limited, Mumbai

Contents

PART 1: CAUSES

CHAPTER 1

The Epidemic of Unfinished Everything and Its Consequences

Have you ever had trouble finishing something, a project at work, or something more personal such as a book, or even a diet? You're not alone. In fact, there's an epidemic of a "failure to finish" syndrome sabotaging not only our lives but the world we live in.

What's behind this epidemic? There are multiple causes. As my research over three decades into time management confirms: one reason is that too many of us are doing too much at once which is leading to the unfinished tasks or projects syndrome that led you to pick up this book.

The second is something I call "distractionitis." People who suffer from this are too easily distracted and are effortlessly pulled away from one task, to do something else. Before you know it, you soon find yourself with too many unfinished jobs or projects. Those unfinished responsibilities start to pile up and you feel overwhelmed. If this happens at work, you could not only be sabotaging yourself but your entire team. It could even put you at risk of being fired.

In our personal lives the effects of failing to finish may be subtler than in the business world, but there are consequences, nevertheless. You never got around to remodeling the bathroom which makes it that much harder to put your house on the market. You moved in a while ago, but there are still unpacked boxes. If only you could lose that last ten pounds, you could finally fit into your wardrobe.

In a survey, over 200 men and women were asked about the #1 project or task that they have left unfinished. Here are just some of their answers:

Work- or school-related

- "Making a vision video for the organization"
- "Finishing an online class"
- "Writing a report of my industrial field visit"
- "Completing my degree"
- "Complete the song I'm writing"
- "Writing a novel"
- "Finding a new job"
- "Doing my lesson plan two weeks ahead"

Personal

- "Paying off my daughter's fees at school"
- "Spending more time with my grandson"
- "Losing weight"
- "Emptying my house of useless stuff"
- "Getting married"

If you find it easier to start rather than finish a project, you are not alone there either. Of the 205 men and women that I queried about that preference, 39 percent wrote that it is easier to start a project; only 19.51 percent wrote that it is easier to finish. When I separated out the 49 respondents from India and the 105 from throughout the United States, the answers were quite consistent: Forty percent of the Americans versus 36.7 percent of the Indians noted that starting is easier than finishing.

There was a third possible answer and that answer received about the same number who wrote that starting is easier than finishing; forty percent (40%) from both countries wrote that it depends on the project. So, for almost half of those who responded to my survey, the challenge relates to a specific task rather than a more global problem with finishing although, as we have seen, for 39% finishing *is* difficult.

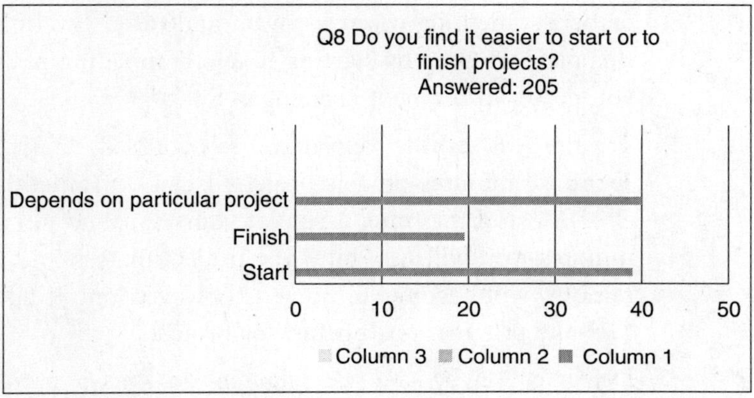

Starting

Although most people in my survey had the most trouble with finishing a project, or, alternatively, it depended on the project, a minority of nearly 20 percent find starting the most challenging.

It's a no brainer that you can't finish a project unless you start, so let's address those occasions when getting started is tougher for you.

I am personally faced with that situation right now. In this case, it's doing the final rewrite on a book I've been working on for a decade. When I initially finished it two years ago, I had been working on it, nonstop, for several months. I had a momentum. But when I stopped and put the book aside, I lost that momentum. It has truly been challenging to get back to the project and finalize it. So, in this case, it is a problem with restarting a project.

So, let's address both situations. Starting and restarting.

If you are having a hard time starting a project or a task:

1. Remind yourself that only by starting will you be able to finish.

2. Is there something you really want to do after you finish this project? Only by starting it, and completing it, can you go on to the next challenge.
3. Try the "just a little" approach. Tell yourself, "If I just spend 10 minutes on this project, I can do something else." Most of the time, if you let yourself spend just 10 minutes, you will get "into" the project or task and 10 minutes will become an hour or however long it takes to make progress on this task or project.
4. Delegate. Maybe you are reluctant to start a project because you should not be doing it in the first place. It is not making the most of your best skills or you are not the right person for the job. You just might be better off passing along the task to someone else.
5. Review all the behaviors and attitudes that you will learn about as possible reasons for failing to finish something and apply it to starting instead. That includes fear of success, fear of failure, procrastination, perfectionism, etc.

The goal of *How to Finish Everything You Start* is to explore the causes, and the possible cures, for the failure to finish syndrome and then empower you to get better at finishing every task or project that you decide you want to finish.

In Chapter 2, we will explore the 22 beliefs, behaviors, and bad habits that are obstacles to finishing.

In Part 3 of this book, we will also discuss making the judgment calls about what you should be working on in the first place. Here we'll explore how failing to finish something might be a test, that there may be a valid reason behind this incompletion, a reason that needs to be assessed, and addressed, before finishing, to make sure finishing is the best course of action.

How to Finish Everything You Start teaches you how to complete more tasks and projects than ever before, empowering you to get more done. By reducing or eliminating the pile of unfinished tasks or endeavors, and all the feelings of self-doubt, lowered self-esteem and self-loathing that too often accompany having unfinished projects, you will become more productive. That will lead to greater success and happiness.

One of the reasons I wrote this book is because I sometimes battle with this issue. It happened again with this book, which I had put off finishing. Once I conducted the final survey and put working on the book into my calendar, making my commitment to the project concrete, to my amazement, the words just flowed.

How to Finish Everything You Start is my seventh time management book starting with *Creative Time Management*, published in 1984 by Prentice Hall and, most recently, *Put More Time on Your Side*, 2nd edition, published in the U.S. and Canada by Sound Wisdom, with foreign rights handled by my small press, Hannacroix Creek Books, Inc.

Six of those books were dedicated to the basic principles of time management including a training manual on teaching time management to IT professionals, *Delivering Time Management to IT Professionals*, published by Packt of Birmingham, England.

Two books are hybrid time management books in that each one applies time management to a specific challenge: finding a romantic partner (*125 Ways to Meet the Love of Your Life*) and the weight challenge (*The Fast Track Guide to Losing Weight and Keeping it Off*). One or more of my time management books have been translated into 15 languages including Spanish, Portuguese, Arabic, Indonesian, simplified and complex Chinese, Korean, Japanese, Slovenian, Croatian, Marathi, Bulgarian, Vietnamese, Russian, and Thai, with Tamil and Hindi translations in preparation.

How to Use This Book

You could read the book straight through and then go back and do the exercises at the end of each chapter or you could read the book one chapter at a time, doing the exercises as you go along. If you prefer, you could also skip the exercises, but you may get more out of it if you make the time to do the accompanying exercises.

A note about library or audiobook editions of this book: Please note: If you have borrowed this book from the library, you have permission to copy any pages that ask you to write down your answers, whether within each chapter, in the Exercises, or in the Appendix. You have permission from the author to photocopy those pages, so you can write down your answers without putting those answers into the library copy. If you buy the book, you are free to write in your own book! If you are listening to this book as an audiobook, we plan to create a packet that you can access after you have purchased the audiobook, so you can download those materials if you choose to write in those exercises.

Consequences of Failing to Finish

Here are a few national and international consequences related to the failing to finish epidemic.

- In the United States, nearly 600,000 high school students drop out annually instead of finishing their degree.
- Almost 50 percent—nearly half—of all American college students will drop out without an undergraduate degree.
- In Venezuela, Mexico, and Chile, only 19 percent of students finished college in 2015.
- Ph.D. candidates drop out at alarming rates becoming what is known as an ABD—All but Dissertation. (According to Rebecca Schuman, in her article, "ABD

Company," that the 10-year completion rate ranges from 49 percent in the humanities to 56 percent in the social sciences and 55-64 percent in the STEM (Science Technology Engineering Mathematics) categories).

Those are just four academic examples of failing to finish what you start that can have a dramatic impact on someone's education, career, wallet, and even someone's self-esteem. There are many others. You probably have a few of your own. Fortunately, *How to Finish Everything You Start* will help you to better understand why this happens and what to do about it, so you finish more often.

Before I share an overview of what you will find in *How to Finish Everything You Start,* I invite you to take a short self-quiz, "Do You Have a Finishing Challenge?"

SELF-QUIZ

Could your ability to finish use improvement?

Take this short 10-question self-evaluation to determine where you stand on the all-important time management skill of finishing. On a piece of paper, or on your computer, answer each question with a yes or no.

1. Do you currently have at least one task, project, or even relationship concern that is unfinished?

   Yes ☐ No ☐

2. Do you have to ask for extensions to any deadlines at work?

   Yes ☐ No ☐ Sometimes ☐

3. Do you ever feel as if you take longer to finish a task than it requires?

   Yes ☐ No ☐ Sometimes ☐

4. Have you or anyone you work for or that is close to you ever called you a perfectionist?

   Yes ☐ No ☐ Sometimes ☐

5. Do you take enough time to do the necessary background research or assessing to make sure what you are working on right now is the best use of your time?

   Yes ☐ No ☐ Sometimes ☐

6. Is there even one task, project, or relationship that is unfinished that is important to you but not necessarily key to your job or others that remains unfinished?

   Yes ☐ No ☐ Sometimes ☐

7. Do you feel as if you currently have too much to do at once?

   Yes ☐ No ☐ Sometimes ☐

8. Do you procrastinate?

   Yes ☐ No ☐ Sometimes ☐

9. Do you daily check your smartphone more than necessary for your job or personal relationships?

   Yes ☐ No ☐ Sometimes ☐

10. Do you say "yes" when you wish you said "no"?

    Yes ☐ No ☐ Sometimes ☐

Review your answers. If you answer *yes* to nine questions, except for number 5, on these ten issues you have challenges related to finishing. (A *yes* to question #5, about doing the necessary research before you commit to something would be the preferred answer.)

If you answered *no* to one or more questions, excluding

question #5, at least on those issues your time management skills related to finishing are excellent.

If you answered *sometimes* answers to any or all these 10 questions, at least in those areas that are important time management skills related to finishing, you could use improvement.

Finishing is an essential skill for those who want to get things done and to be more successful and productive. I think of an editor who got fired years ago from the book publisher where he had been working for several years because he was so afraid of making the wrong decisions that he failed to finish any of the deals he initiated.

Your reputation at work depends on you finishing what you are asked to do and completing it on time within the agreed-upon deadline, whenever possible.

Fortunately, in the chapters ahead, you will hopefully find help for yourself so that you become a much more efficient and consistent finisher.

What's Ahead in This Book

There are four additional chapters in Part 1 following this chapter: Causes.

Chapter 2, "The Reasons Are Within You: 22 Beliefs, Behaviors, or Bad Habits That May Be Stopping You from Finishing" goes through all the possible reasons you are quitting, from fear or failure or success, to perfectionism, procrastination, and lots more. Like all the subsequent chapters, Chapter 2 ends with exercises to reinforce what you learned.

In Chapter 3, "Having Too Much to Do at Once," we will explore the number one reason people give for not finishing. There just seems too much to do!

Chapter 4, "Dealing with Procrastination," addresses how

mastering your procrastination tendency just might be the way that you finish more often, and faster. You may have read about procrastination before, but this is a new approach. I have previously advocated creative procrastination and I will explain what that is—putting aside one priority task to do another rather than just wasting time when you're blocked on doing something—but the growth of unfinished tasks and projects is, sadly, one of the consequences if creative procrastination is misused or inappropriately applied on a continual basis. Because of that in this chapter I advocate the more conservative "one thing at a time" method of getting things done.

In the last chapter in Part 1, Chapter 5, "Rethinking Deadlines," I explore how deadlines are a blessing rather than something to be dreaded. Deadlines keep us on track and motivate us to finish in a more organized way.

Part 2, "Cures," addresses more solutions to your failure to finish challenge. There are six chapters in this part. These cover specific techniques to help you finish any project. In Chapter 6, "Using F-I-N-I-S-H," you will learn about the acronym F-I-N-I-S-H and how to use it to complete your key projects.

Chapter 7, "Taking Control: Goal Setting and Prioritizing," helps you with an up-to-date perspective on the importance of setting, and clarifying, short- and long-term goals. I review the SMART acronym for goal setting for those familiar with that powerful goal-setting tool; introducing it to you if you are unfamiliar with it till now.

Chapter 8, "To-Do Lists That Work," provides you with another cure for failing to finish: gaining clarity on just what you need to do each day. To-do lists are a way to break up larger projects into smaller more manageable ones.

Chapter 9, "Learning to Say No," is about another typical behavior pattern that gets those with finishing challenges into further trouble. So, learning how to say no graciously is a way to remedy that situation.

In Chapter 10, "Becoming a Better Delegator," you learn another powerful tool to get more projects and tasks finished, namely delegating. In addition to doing too many things at once, trying to do everything yourself is another big problem. Learning to delegate is a powerful tool that can free up your time to focus on finishing what you are best at. Who should you delegate to and how can you be an effective delegator are key concerns. Delegating to people is an obvious way to delegate but you can also delegate to technology, saving time and freeing up energy and focus. What technology can work and how do you know it's an asset and not making you more frustrated and time starved?

The last chapter in Part 2 is Chapter 11, "An Example of Finally Finishing a Major Effort: Writing a Book." In this chapter, I present a detailed approach to overcoming the tendency to stop a book project before it is finished and published. By focusing on this one common unfinished task for so many aspiring, new, and even seasoned authors, you will see how even something as potentially complicated and long term as a book project can be finished once you figure out what is behind the delays and you do something about it.

Part 3, "Further Thoughts and Conclusion," has two chapters: Chapter 12, "The Exception That Proves the Rule: When Failing to Finish Is Beneficial" and Chapter 13, "Concluding Thoughts." What is key in Chapter 12 is the emphasis on you making conscious choices about what to finish, and even when to complete things, rather than letting your unconscious resistances or bad habits put tasks or projects on the back burner that should be completed.

Finally, in "Concluding Thoughts" in addition to exploring what your life could be like if you selectively finished everything you started, I address some of the sources of help that you might consider exploring. For example, if you think you have adult ADHD, which can lead to failing to finish projects, you might want to seek out medical help and even consider medication that could help you control your ADHD. If you think that you should work with a project manager, I will discuss that possibility. Finally, the conclusion ends with you envisioning what your life could be life if you selectively finish everything you start as we go on a "what if" journey as you continue working toward a more productive you.

In "Selected Bibliography Including Cited Works" you will find the complete citations for any articles or books mentioned throughout this text as well as additional related books, articles, or even videos that you might find useful to pursue.

In the "Resources" section, you will find a list of related associations, organizations, or companies as well as some of the more popular technology available for helping you to manage your projects.

The "Appendix" includes blanks of the ACTION! Strategy Worksheet, an acronym to help you with prioritizing, as well as sample to-do lists that you might want to use or adapt. *How to Finish Everything You Start* concludes with "About the Author" which describes my credentials in greater detail as well as how you can contact me if you are interested in attending one of my workshops, getting coached, or subscribing to my free mailing list for announcements about future books, blog posts, or upcoming author appearances.

EXERCISES

1. Circle, highlight, or check off all the reasons that you want to learn to finish everything or at least selectively finish what you care about more often and more efficiently. After you circle the phrases or words that describe the benefits of learning to be a better finisher, keep this list as a reminder of your motivation to finish reading this book and improving the time management skill of finishing.

Feeling good	Feeling more organized
Being more productive	Accomplishing more
Having more personal time	Being further in my career
Feeling less stressed	Making more money
Being more organized	Being more successful
Having a less chaotic life	Getting higher grades
Work is stress-free	Being less worried
Developing a reputation as a finisher	Other ________________
Being happier	Other ________________
	Other ________________

Keep those circled or checked off motivators as a record of how you predict finishing more often will make you feel. After you have read this book, done some or all the exercises, and put into practice some of the recommendations, as well as applied any insights into yourself to unfinished projects so that you selectively are finishing more projects or tasks in your best interest, see how your projections stack up to how you feel or your performance at your job.

2. Since lack of focus and "distractionitis" are contributing to the failure to finish epidemic, are you aware of how often you check your own smartphone, if you have one? If you lack a smartphone, how often do you check e-mail on the Internet or, if you are on social media, such as Facebook, LinkedIn, Instagram, or Pinterest, how frequently are you checking those accounts? Take the time to monitor yourself for at least an hour or two or even for 12 hours or an entire 24 hours/one day. In addition to how often you check social media, see if you may also track how much time you spend on it in one sitting.

Frequency of checking my smartphone

______ Within 30 minutes

______ Within 1 hour

______ With 2 hours

______ Within 12 hours

Frequency of and length of time spent on social media

Social media	How often checked in 1-hour	Time spent daily
Facebook	______________	______________
LinkedIn	______________	______________
Instagram	______________	______________
Pinterest	______________	______________
Snapchat	______________	______________
Twitter	______________	______________

CHAPTER 2

The Reasons Are Within You: 22 Beliefs, Behaviors, or Bad Habits That May Be Stopping You from Finishing

In my research, I've identified 22 behaviors, beliefs, or bad habits that stop us from finishing what we start.

1. Fear of failure
2. Fear of success
3. Perfectionism
4. Fear of completion
5. Procrastination (covered in depth in chapter 4)
6. Poor planning
7. Poor pacing
8. Setting an unrealistic deadline in the first place
9. Taking on too many tasks (another vital reason that will also get its own chapter 3)
10. Disorganization
11. Emotional turmoil
12. Anger
13. Working under pressure backfires
14. Allowing yourself to stop at a certain point and temporarily quit
15. "Out of sight, out of mind"—a task is not looming in front of you
16. Starting a new task even before finishing the one you were working on
17. TV, videogaming, social media, the Internet, or other distractions
18. Having a problem with lateness

19. Devaluing yourself or your goal
20. Overvaluing yourself or your goal
21. Failing to plan for, or allow, interruptions
22. Being too inconsistent in your effort

Fear of failure

If you don't finish a task or project, you can't fail. This way of thinking, which could be conscious or unconscious, may be preventing you from finishing. The sad part of this fear is that by failing to finish, you bring about the very failure that you fear. You could have written the most wonderful report in the world. But if your boss asked you to hand it in tomorrow and you need another week, or more, to complete it, the reaction will usually be less than favorable even if you are granted more time.

Where does fear of failure come from? It often begins early in life. A child is told that a 95 is not good enough. A teen gets the message that the college he or she is applying to could have been a better ranked one. Instead of a parent, teacher or any authority figure building up the child's self-esteem they are taught to feel like a failure by being told they always fall short of what's expected of them. This becomes one lesson they learn all too well.

If this sounds familiar, it may be the reason you're blocked on finishing a task or project. What can you do about it?

First, imagine the worst thing that might happen once you complete the project. Imagine yourself being told that you need to redo it, or finding out that someone else got the award, and not you.

Can you see yourself surviving that disappointment? Can you see yourself coping with that bad news?

Now, try to alter your projections about what might happen if told that your report is excellent. See yourself getting the award, winning it over 78 other applicants.

Can you cope with this good news?

Now think about somewhere in between those two extremes. You are told your report needs work, but your boss is confident you can redo the report as needed. You did not get the award, but you are encouraged to apply again next year.

Like with all these 22 behaviors, beliefs, or bad habits, recognizing that you have one or more is the first step. If self-talk or working hard on your own to sort out why this time waster is stopping you from finishing, is not working, consider working with a therapist. If this is a long-standing trait and tendency, it might be time to focus in on the underlying causes that are holding you back.

Fear of failure is such a typical reason to quit or leave something unfinished that I want to offer some possible solutions for dealing with this belief:

1 Get the training and experience that will give you confidence.

If you're competent, you're less likely to fail. By reinforcing your abilities to succeed, you will be more confident about going forward and finishing.

2 Imagine the worst consequence of finishing and see yourself overcoming it.

In my book, *The Fast Track Guide to Speaking in Public*, I share 12 of the worst speaking situations. I offer the same advice that I have just given: see yourself dealing with each one of those scenarios and surviving. What are those possibilities? Everything from having the entire audience walk out on you to forgetting what you want to say next to being heckled by one or numerous audience members. Those are just some of the situations that every speaker has had to deal with.

But surviving those tough situations, and continuing to

speak, separates the amateurs from the professionals. Similarly, whatever it is that you are failing to finish, if you can see yourself dealing with criticism, or whatever it is that is your worst fear that might come from finishing, you can get the courage to push forward, and finish.

Maybe you are afraid to graduate because you don't know if you'll get a job. Can you deal with that? You can because at least you'll have your degree. Maybe you are afraid if you finish your book and it gets published, you might get a negative review or two. Can you live with that? Think of all the great books that had some or a lot of criticism at first, such as Herman Melville's masterpiece *Moby Dick*.

3 See failure as a badge of courage, change how you view it.

There's a cliché that goes something like, "We fail toward success."

It takes failure to finally triumph. Elsewhere in this book I use the fable Thomas Edison about Thomas Edison trying and failing 1,000 times before he discovered the world-changing light bulb. There are so many more examples. A quick Google search on failures who finally made it brings up the tales of Walt Disney, who supposedly was turned down 302 times for financing for his epic theme park, or billionaire J.K. Rowling of Harry Potter fame who was close to being homeless and whose initial novel was rejected 12 times before finding a publisher.

You might succeed with whatever it is that you are delaying finishing, but the key point is that you'll never know unless you have the courage to keep going and get it out there.

4 Be realistic about whatever it is that is not working in whatever you are putting off and make those changes.

If you're afraid that whatever you're delaying might lead to failure, that might be a good fear because it could be highlighting that you need to make changes, do more work, or take another approach. Instead of fearing failure, critically reassess your task or project and, if you think there is reason that you might fail, make those changes so success is more likely.

5 Consider failing as a training ground for succeeding.

There is another adage about that it is not whether you get knocked down that matters but whether you get up again afterwards. If you don't finish and cannot get judged, how will you develop that strength to keep going?

6 If you do not finish, you bring out the very failure that you fear.

Quitting or failing to finish is a type of failure, perhaps the worst kind since it is failure by default. If you want to stop, and consciously make that choice, that is one thing. But if you simply cease to try, or quit by passively shelving something or even someone, you are not being proactive about your career or your life.

Fear of Success

This is the opposite side of the same coin of the fear of failure but it is more insidious and unfortunately has a similar outcome: it immobilizes you so that you cannot finish a task or project and submit it.

Why would someone fear success? If you grew up feeling as if you were the "smart one" or the "better athlete" than your siblings, and that made you feel guilty about your achievements, you might be reluctant to turn in a project, or complete a task, because you have mixed feelings about shining. You may fear that you will make your co-workers look bad if you are the one who is praised over their accomplishments.

If you have a father or mother who felt like he or she did not attain what he or she wanted to do accomplish in his or her life, finishing a project may bring up those old fears that you will outshine your senior relative.

Those are the potential deep-rooted causes of a fear of success, but it might be more on the surface, as noted above, whereby you are afraid you will upstage your co-workers, or, even worse, your boss.

So, you delay, avoiding success.

Sadly, most of the time, delays bring about the opposite of success: condemnation, criticism, and disappointment. If that is more comfortable for you, then by failing to complete a task or project, you are providing yourself with those unconscious "rewards" which, are punishments.

As with the fear of failure syndrome, you need to do a lot of soul searching and self-talk to push yourself to go beyond these emotional traps that stop you from finishing and getting the praise, or at least the feedback, that you deserve and need.

Perfectionism

I want my surgeon and my proofreader to be perfectionists. For most others, aiming for excellence that is attainable is a better use of our time than striving for a perfectionism that is unrealistic. How does being a perfectionist stop you from finishing something? The perfectionist redoes and redoes something again and again trying to get it "just right." Rewriting an e-mail so it has the right information or tone, or revising a pitch so it's more effective, are not time wasters. When your efforts are becoming a time waster is when you are putting into the task time, energy, and other skills that are disproportionate to the outcome or benefits.

We must go back to childhood and teen years to see the causes of perfectionism. The parent or teacher who could not be pleased. The father or mother who said that 99 was not good enough. It had to be 100. The B+ that got berated because it was not an A. Unfortunately, these kinds of messages during the formative years stay with someone. It is key to recognize that it is those kinds of unrealistic standards that are making you afraid to finish.

That does not mean that you turn in a sloppy report, or that you do not proofread your essay to make sure there are no spelling or grammatical errors or typos. But it does mean that you learn to let go when it is time to let go. When you have tried your best and it is time to submit your efforts. You might want to share what you are doing with others to get feedback and to ensure that what you are finishing is your best effort. But making sure something is your best effort is not the same thing as delaying yourself days, weeks, months, or even years because it might be an imperfect whatever—book, play, business plan, revised website—the list goes on and on.

Here are some solutions if your perfectionism is stopping you from finishing:

1 Realize that you are a perfectionist.

As with any time waster, or bad habit, the first step is to see that this trait describes you. Without putting yourself down or judging yourself, now that you realize you are a perfectionist, and it is causing you to have a finishing challenge, what will you do about it?

2 Accept that no one, including you, is perfect.

Now that you have recognized that you are a perfectionist, you need to accept yourself as the imperfect person that you are so that you will control your urge to keep going with a task or project beyond what is appropriate for the situation. In other words, you rewrite an e-mail a dozen times even though it was fine after the second rewrite. Or you want to write the perfect blog but by reworking it beyond the excellent result you already achieved you delay finishing it and miss the opportunity to comment on a timely issue.

These affirmations may be helpful:

> "I am imperfect."
>
> "I love myself the way I am."
>
> "I am comfortable aiming for excellence."

3 Learn to be comfortable with praise or accepting of feedback that might be negative.

Perfectionists who keep going so that they fail to finish may be afraid of getting criticized for their less-than-perfect efforts or, if they are used to being imperfect, may be uncomfortable with the subsequent praise that follow finishing. Work on being at ease with either type of feedback situation.

4 Readjust your standards to strive for attainable excellence rather than unrealistic perfection.

As mentioned before, setting your sights on excellent achievements that are attainable could free a perfectionist up from the unworkable standards to underly quitting or having unfinished efforts.

5 Delegate or partner with others.

If you are too hard on yourself, having someone else do some or all of a task, or even partnering with someone who takes over responsibility for the completion of a project, might help you to move things along to a successful conclusion.

6 Remind yourself that perfectionism has its consequences.

Bosses who seem to never be pleased because they are perfectionists may be unwittingly creating a hostile work environment where subordinates feel nothing they do is ever enough. Instead of feeling motivated to reach the perfectionistic high standards that the boss is setting, the workers feel defeated and undermined. They may start looking for a new job, or request a transfer to another department where their excellent efforts will be recognized and rewarded. If you are a perfectionist in a position of authority, you risk being labeled as such, a trait that human resources or the leadership will most likely see as a negative trait in the workplace.

Parents who are pushing their children or teens, or even judging their grown children, by perfectionist standards need to realize how they may be causing deep-seated feelings of insecurity as they impose unattainable perfectionistic benchmarks on their offspring.

In personal relationships, applying perfectionistic standards to your friends or romantic partners can also sabotage what could be a wonderful connection. Accept imperfection in those you care about as well as yourself.

Fear of Completion

Poor self-esteem and insecurity may be at the core of a fear of completion that stops you from finishing. If you have a perfectionism issue, you may fear completing something because it will not be perfect enough. As long as you delay completing it, you can keep reworking it, avoiding the negative feedback that you dread.

Apply to your fear of completion these questions: what is my inability to complete something doing for me emotionally? What are the conscious or unconscious benefits from this behavior? If I were to complete something, what might the outcome be, positive or negative? Can I see myself facing that on my own or do I need some help? Perhaps you were raised by parents who made you feel that nothing you ever do is good enough. Perhaps you had teachers who did not praise you enough even if it was earned.

Your fear of completion might be tied to a fear that you will be bored when you finish a particular task or project, especially if it is a major, all-consuming one, you worry about what you will do next. A way to work around that fear of boredom, as long as you avoid the doing-too-much-at-once trap, is to have at least one task or project lined up that you will do when this commitment is completed.

If you are worried about how your finished project or task will be evaluated, you may be putting it off, or switching to something else, to delay what you fear will accompany completing something. You may find some useful suggestions with how to deal with the procrastination that would follow in the section below.

Procrastination

(Covered briefly here and in more detail in Chapter 4)

Procrastination is a huge time waster that stops someone from finishing. But just saying that, or acknowledging that, does not really help. I see procrastination different than most. I see procrastination as *information*. Why are you delaying? What is the putting off of a project telling you? Is it that the project was not the right one to be working on in the first place? Is it that you really need to be addressing something else first and this project, the one you think you are procrastinating about, is just less of a priority so it must wait?

What I think will serve you well if you think you have a procrastination problem is to really probe what is behind the delaying. Sometimes procrastination slows you down, so you can reevaluate something to make sure that you should be working on a project in the first place. Perhaps someone else in your department should be working on the report that you agreed to do? You may be procrastinating because you are angry and resentful about being asked to do something that is someone else's job, or work that is too simple or even too difficult for you to handle.

Like each one of these 22 behaviors, beliefs, or bad habits that are stopping you from finishing, you need to figure out why you are procrastinating. But make it specific. Just labeling yourself a procrastinator is not going to help anyone, especially you. Get beyond that label to look at the specifics.

What is the thing you need to finish that you are putting off finishing (procrastinating about)? Write down a brief description.

____

List at least one, or up to three, reasons that you might be delaying.

Reason #1 ____________________________________

Reason #2 ____________________________________

Reason #3 ____________________________________

Now consider each of those reasons for the delay. Is there a pattern to those reasons? Is there a logic to what's causing you to put off finishing?

Now list the consequences of procrastinating on finishing this specific task or project:

Consequence #1 ________________________________

Consequence #2 ________________________________

Consequence #3 ______________________________

Now that you know the potential consequences of failing to finish, consider how you might reward yourself for finishing.

Reward #1 ___________________________________

What reward did you write? Going to the movies? Going out to dinner? Buying yourself a new computer?

Poor planning

Poor planning is part of what I refer to as the 4Ps of delay and inefficiency – procrastination, perfectionism, poor planning, and poor pacing.

Poor planning is often not the same thing as not being aware of just what is going to be involved in a project. By contrast, poor planning usually boils down to underestimating the time something will take. If you agree to a new project based on the assumption of when the first project will be completed, if you did not plan well, and the first project takes longer, before you know it, you can have one, two, three projects stacked up. I became especially sensitive to this challenge when I was conducting the interviews with IT professionals of all levels – from programmers to CEOs – for my training manual, *Delivering Time management to IT Professionals*. The grave consequences of underestimating how long an IT project might take is dramatically highlighted in the book, *Death March* by Edward Yourdon. Yourdon defines death march as a software project whereby "the schedule has been compressed to less than half the amount of time estimated by a rational estimating process; thus, the project that would normally be expected to take 12 calendar months is now required to be delivered in six months or less."

Why, you might ask, does someone agree to a project and a

deadline that is half or even more than half the amount of time that it should take? There are lots of reasons. One obvious reason is that if the project manager – possibly you – told someone how long a project might take, whether it's a longer-term project, like a book, or even writing a business plan or doing an evaluation of a program, you might consciously or unconsciously fear that the work will be given to someone else, who agrees to a much shorter time frame. Or the new project might be so unique that you really are clueless about how long it is going to take so your estimate is way off.

Another scenario is that when you agreed to a certain deadline, you had less on your plate at the time. You thought it would be smooth sailing to plan that you needed x amount of time to deliver y. But, life happens and suddenly your planned completion date comes up short.

If this is a one-time thing, it is obviously going to be a lot easier to explain and deal with than if it is a pattern of behavior that causes you to get labeled as a poor planner.

So how can you go from being a poor planner to an accurate or excellent planner?

Here are some suggestions:

Promise less, deliver more. Keep expectations low or lower and come in ahead of those expectations so you look like a super performer rather than an underachiever.

If you have done a similar project before, how long did that take?

If there are differences between this and the other project or projects, what are those variations? Will that add or subtract the necessary time you need to get the project finished?

If this is a completely new project, so you lack something comparable to compare it to in terms of scheduling, is there another project that is at least somewhat similar that you could use so you have some information to work with? What are the differences or distinctions between these projects that cause you to add or subtract time from your estimate?

Planning should be conscious and considered. It should not be something that you pick out of thin air because it sounds like a nice time frame to commit to.

The more you base the delivery date for a task or project on research and an assessment of your previous performance, the more likely you are to make or beat the submission dates that you set for yourself.

There is another rule in time management. Whatever time you think something is going to take, add 25 percent to give yourself enough time to complete a project on time. Sometimes you may even want to add 50 percent.

There is that maxim that things will expand to the time that is allowed for it as if having too much time can be a bad thing. If you are adding time that is unnecessary, since so many projects and tasks do depend on getting to market as fast as possible, frivolously adding time can backfire.

Most of all, take time in your planning. Sometimes it is what you do at the very beginning of a project, or even before that project begins, that can determine how smoothly it will go and whether you will meet or beat your deadline days, weeks, months, or even years down the road.

Oftentimes the more planning you do at the beginning of a project, the better it will go and the greater the likelihood it will end well. As a married Ph.D. student at a university in Thailand put it, "I think one of the biggest [time management challenges] is that many people do not realize that spending time on preparation of large projects or tasks beforehand saves a great deal of time when it's time to actually do it."

Poor pacing

You usually can't write an entire book in a day, a week, or even a month and you certainly need to take breaks throughout your day. So, pacing on a daily or regular basis can make or break not just whether you finish something in a timely fashion but in what shape you finish something physically, mentally, and emotionally.

The reason Yourdon wrote his book, *Death March*, published by Prentice Hall in 1997, is that poor pacing on software projects happens too often. Poor pacing is not just an IT or software developer's problem. Look at so many industries where figuring out how long something will take is so challenging that it leads to pulling all-nighters, not just for college students but for those working in offices, trying to stay awake by drinking lots of caffeine-rich beverages.

Remember to consider the daily pacing to see realistically just how much work you can get done in any given day and the longer-term pacing, of how long a project or task is going to take.

Setting an unrealistic deadline in the first place

Assuming life or work challenges, or additional projects, have not gotten piled on top of you, if you set a realistic deadline in the first place, you would probably not be in the failure to finish situation. If it is too late to set a realistic deadline for the project or task you're already working on, be reassured that there is help, and hope, for you in the future.

What makes a deadline realistic? As noted before, you need to know how long you think something is going to take. You could base it on how long it took to finish similar projects previously or, if that is not the case, at least piecing together a prediction based on bits and pieces of other related tasks or projects that you or others have done. You can even do some research by polling others who have been in a similar situation or doing a Google search on whatever it is that you're working on. There are varieties in how long people take to do everything and anything, from writing or editing, to making phone calls or even preparing a master contact list of speakers for the annual meeting that you're organizing.

You just want to be preparing a deadline based on research and experience rather than picking a date out of thin air or trying to please someone else, so you agree to their date without thinking through whether it will work for you.

Taking on too many tasks

(another vital reason that will also get its own chapter, Chapter 3)

The entire next chapter is devoted to doing too much at once since this, according to a survey I administered, is the number one reason behind a failure to finish. If you agree to do five tasks, or projects, and you really can only work on one at a time, and have the resources, energy, and focus to work on one, or two at the most, you will soon find yourself with too many unfinished projects or responsibilities.

What is interesting to me is that when I did a survey of 234 working men and women about the #1-time waster that they were dealing with, 33 percent gave "trying to do too much at once" as the reason. The second through fifth reasons, which were virtually tied at eight percent were: procrastination, an inability to say "no," too much paperwork, and perfectionism.

Doing too much at once is the biggest challenge to managing your time and getting things done. Consider the mail situation today. In the "old days," you would get letters that you could put into an inbox, reading those letters when it was convenient for you. There were some who would jump to open a letter out of curiosity about who it was from, but in most cases, regular mail was a much more manageable situation.

Now consider the situation for most of us today. Mail is

delivered electronically on our smartphones. A study by SWNS (South West News Service), posted at the New York Post, reported that "Americans check their phones 80 times a day." That translates into once every 12 minutes. The survey of 2,000 people found that one in 10 checks their smartphone every four minutes.

Whether or not someone reads the mail that he or she finds when that check occurs, it is still a much more distracted situation leading to feeling pulled in more directions than when you could store your mail somewhere until you had time to go through it.

Just reading through e-mails is a form of taking on too many tasks. But in the next chapter, we will look at even the bigger picture when it comes to taking on too many tasks. (The cure, "Learning to Say 'No,'" will be explored in Chapter 9 in Part 2, "Cures.") In the next chapter, we will delve into taking on too many tasks as one of the causes of not finishing what you have started.

Disorganization

How does disorganization tie in with not finishing what you started? You can't finish something if you can't even find what you're supposed to be doing in the first place.

Disorganization is also tied to clutter. If you have piles and piles of papers, and books, and files, and you failed to put away the file that contains the project that you are working on, it is going to be hard to find that project, and to work on it in a timely fashion. You may be tempted to jump to another project, so you are at least working on something rather than just going through your desk or bookshelves embarrassing yourself by the disorganized mess you call your office.

There is, fortunately, hope for the time waster of disorganization. We will deal with that in Chapter 6, "Taking Control and

Prioritizing." Taking control is more than just taking control of what projects you are working on, or the work that you commit to. It is also taking control of your workspace and outside the office or, if you telecommute, to the office that you work in at home.

Emotional turmoil

It's hard to finish projects when you're emotionally upset. That emotional turmoil can be because of your own situation, such as a friend's husband passing away, or a relative having health problems, or it can be relationship challenges or even financial trials that pull your concentration and energy away from the projects at hand.

Unfortunately, as much as possible, you need to muster your emotional strength to push on to get done what needs to be done. In many businesses or professions today, time is of the essence and time is not just money, but time is everything. If you must take a personal day, or even a week or more, then that's what you must do. But keep track of what's going on with yourself so that you get the help you need if your emotional turmoil persists so long that you're trying the patience of your team, company, or even your own need to find a calm that will render you not just more productive but happier.

If you find it hard to stick with things because you need immediate gratification, it can lead to not finishing something. Sometimes you might say "yes" to something without being completely sure of just how much effort is involved. As you get into the project, and you realize there is more work to it than you imagined, you might not be able to delegate some or all of the work. You just might have to do it yourself and learn from this experience.

One way to deal with this is to break up a big task into more manageable little tasks. That could help someone with low frustration tolerance. You just have to do each little task rather than the overwhelming big one.

Low-frustration tolerance or impatience often has a long history so it's a tendency not easily overturned or changed. But it is something to be aware of and to be careful about in the workplace especially since it can hold you back from having the positive record of completion that will take you far.

If you have a problem with impatience, the first step is to be aware of it. The next step is to learn to work in self-contained units so you avoid getting too exhausted or overwhelmed so that you start losing temper or making mistakes.

If you find yourself really frustrated with a more complicated project or task, if possible, you can delegate some aspects of the work to others.

You can also have a set number of ways that you deal with your frustration that are positive and not self-destructive, like overeating or yelling at people, so you can call on one or more of those options, as needed. Taking a walk, meditating, calling or texting a friend (if you do it in a way that does not make others think that you are goofing off at work), listening to music, exercising, reading books or positive articles on the Internet. What are your additional ways of handling frustration?

Anger

Anger gets in the way of completion more often than we'd like to admit. You could be angry at someone you work with or displacing and projecting your anger to the person you'll be submitting a project to, or even the team that is awaiting your material. Whether it is a direct line between you and the angry party or a more convoluted connection, anger is the key element here. Anger is shutting you down. Making you reluctant to finish whatever because you are angry.

What to do? First, you need to recognize that you are angry

and that it might be a cause of your inability to finish. Once you establish that you can consider who you are angry at and why.

Once you figure that out, you need to discuss how you feel with that person, either in person or by phone, if necessary. If you feel uncomfortable or unsafe talking in person, you may have to bring in a third party.

You may even consider roleplay with a substitute what you're going to say. Once you establish a safe situation, just talking it out might free you up. If you do not have anyone to roleplay with, or no one feels comfortable doing this with you, consider self-talk as another option. Self-talk in the privacy of your home into a mirror or talk to an empty chair. But get out everything that is bothering you and possibly preventing you from finishing a project.

Working under pressure backfires

Some people seem to perform better under pressure, but for most of us, working under pressure backfires. You start to feel more stressed than ever before. You might even start making more mistakes or even feeling so overwhelmed by the time pressure that you put your required work aside and take a long walk, or go to a movie, or just throw up your hands in frustration that you are in an intense and unworkable situation.

There is a reason that the adage "slow and steady wins the race" has survived and is still quoted. Because in most cases, it is true. Which takes us back to pacing and planning. Developing, and maintaining, a steady rhythm of performance usually goes a lot further than working in intense spurts.

Allow yourself to stop at a certain point and temporarily quit but only for a set time period, not an open-ended one.

Are you a quitter? You may have never seen yourself in that light but maybe, lately, you are just so overwhelmed by all the demands on you that you take one or more projects to a certain point and then you just put it aside. You think that you're going to get right back to it, but hours become days, and that turns into weeks, months, or maybe even years. This is more likely to be true for projects that you personally care about, rather than the tasks that are assigned to you, by your boss or, if you are a student, by your professor. Ironically these projects or tasks that you put aside just might turn out to be the ones that catapult you to the next level in your career. Maybe it involves going back to school, or applying for a Fulbright Scholarship, or finishing the novel or nonfiction book you have been working on for the last five years.

Why do you stop? What's that about? Go back to the time wasters we discussed earlier in this chapter and see which ones, if any, apply. Could it be the fear of success? Fear of failure? Perfectionism? Poor planning? Procrastination?

Okay, give yourself a little bit of a respite but do not let it drag on and on. Get back on the horse. Recommit to the task and to seeing it through to completion. If you have a solid reason to stop doing something, as discussed further in Chapter 12, "The Exception That Proves the Rule: When Failing to Finish is a Good thing," that's fine. But are you stopping because you are letting yourself off the hook too easily? Perhaps you are running out of steam or just need to get your batteries recharged so you have more motivation to keep going, then find a way to push yourself.

Here are some affirmations you can consider repeating to motivate yourself to get back to the project or task at hand:

"I am doing this project."

"I am completing this task."

"I am a finisher."

"I can handle whatever I need to do."

"Out of sight, out of mind" – a task is not looming in front of you

There are some for whom having a project tucked away in a filing cabinet, or a file that is on the hard drive of a computer, makes it that much harder to see what needs to be done. Putting projects in front of you, or sticking reminders on a bulletin board, looks disorganized and cluttered. So, how do we make what needs to be done concrete but without making everything so visual and distracting that it becomes counterproductive?

Each of us must solve this challenge for ourselves but it is helpful to at least be aware of this phenomenon: "out of sight, out of mind." Having a completely clear and clean desk might impress others, but does it really indicate someone who is productive? When I was conducting interviews for my book, *Making Your Office Work for You,* I interviewed several executives who told me they had two offices: the front office where they greeted visitors and where there was a minimum of clutter because this was, after all, the office for show. Then there was the back office, the place where the "real" work got done. There were files all around, and books, and computers and file cabinets.

In a similar way, I interviewed a psychologist who had a large room where she saw patients. Toward the back of the room, which was furnished very simply with a sofa and her desk and a chair, was an oversized screen. That screen concealed all the clutter behind it. The files and books that the psychologist needed to do her work but that would be a distraction to her patient. It would also send a message of disorder that she was reluctant to communicate.

In Chapter 8, "To Do Lists that Work," we will explore how you can use a to do list to create an orderly way that you remind yourself of all the commitments that you must do, or finish. It could be a handy way to take control while still maintaining the more organized physical office or home office or home spaces that conceal the tasks or projects that you are currently working on.

Starting a new task even before finishing the one you were working on

This is a huge way to find yourself in a bit of a bind with too many projects that are simultaneously due. The good news is that you are not alone if you find it easier to start, rather than finish, a task or project. In my survey of 205 men and women, 39 percent find it easier to start a project than to finish it, only 19.5 percent found it easier to finish, and another 40 percent noted that it depends on the project.

So, if you fall into that first group who find it easier to start a project than complete it, beware of this tendency! You may find yourself saying "yes" and committing to a whole bunch of tasks or projects only to find yourself in a real pickle because you keep starting and not finishing each one up!

Now if you fall into the category of "it depends" on the project, at least there is some consideration as to what project or task is involved. If you can start to get an understanding about what projects are easier to start, than finish, and vice versa, that could help you to get a grip on your tendencies in either direction. You must really work on this tendency.

TV, videogaming, the Internet, e-mail, social media, or other distractions

We already noted how checking one's phone constantly can stop you from doing what you must do. What about watching TV, playing videogames, reading articles unrelated to the project at hand on the Internet, and other distractions? These are most definitely time wasters, especially if done to excess. In moderation, all these distractions can be a nice respite from work, especially if it is done during non-work hours! During work hours, these are time wasters that have no place in the hours when you should be working. But during non-work hours, or on weekends, one or all these activities can be a reward or a way to unwind from the physical or mental work that you usually do.

In my survey of 205 men and women, here are the results of how long those individuals spent checking, or answering, e-mails daily:

"I check my e-mails constantly"	(8%)
1-1/2 to 2 hours	(12%)
1-1/2 hours	(10%)
31-60 minutes	(22%)
11-30 minutes	(20%)
1-10 minutes	(15%)
1-1/2 to 2 hours	(12%)
3 hours	(6%)
4 hours	(.49%)
5 hours	(1%)
6 hours	(2%)

Unless you have a job in customer service, where you must check e-mails constantly, or a similar job that requires continual checking of e-mails, you can see that some of the respondents have a serious problem with e-mail. That includes those who check e-mail constantly (8%) and those who check e-mails for 3-6 hours (8.49%). The others, who check their e-mails from 1-10 minutes to 2 hours, in an 8-hour workday would still be able to get other work done.

In the last chapter you were asked in the Exercises section to monitor how often you check your e-mail as well as how much time you spend on social media. Look over your answers now. Are you spending too much time checking e-mail or on social media, especially during the work day? Is that distracting you and making it harder for you to do the concentrated work that could help you to finish whatever it is that you started that you need to complete to help move your career or even your personal life along?

What is key is not just moderation but being aware of how much time you are spending. You also need to be tuned into what tasks or projects are needing to finish, and when, and to make sure you are making those necessary activities a priority. Prioritizing, one of the cornerstones of time management training and productivity, will take you far in mastering the art of finishing. Chapter 6, "Taking Control and Prioritizing," will probe prioritizing in a more in-depth way.

For now, just be aware that all these activities named above can be time wasters when you are trying to improve the frequency with which you get everything done, "on time and under budget," as they are quoted as saying in Hollywood when they have had a successful movie shoot.

Having a problem with lateness

This chapter on time wasters would not be complete without a discussion about lateness and how that influences failing to finish everything you start or, in many cases, turning things in late.

Lateness is impolite to others. On the rare occasion that it is necessary, because of transit delays, for example, or sudden emergencies, that is one thing. Occasional lateness, especially if it's justified, is usually forgiven and forgivable. But if the lateness is chronic and if the reason is inexplicable, such as "I overslept," or "I forgot to set my alarm," or "I left my house too late," it reflects badly on you and, if others are waiting for you, it inconveniences many who will label you as someone with a lateness problem.

This does tie to the theme of this book, *How to Finish Everything You Start.* Usually, the person who has failed to finish something is running behind or late. With coaxing and reminders, the task or project may eventually get completed and submitted. But it has not been accomplished in the smooth and effortless way that it could have been achieved.

Your delays, which translate into being late, show that you consider yourself and your time more important than others. If you are on the receiving end of that lateness, you know how being kept waiting usually makes you feel. I think the standard amount of time that most people expect to wait for someone in a social situation, such as meeting for lunch, would be fifteen to thirty minutes, unless there was a phone call received explaining that the other party will be even later.

But what about with projects or tasks that are due? How long should someone wait for you? How long should you wait for someone else? What if this person is the absolute best person to do this task and you know that waiting for him or her is better than getting a less impressive effort from someone else, who might be on time? Those are, questions you must ask, and answer, but what about the ideal combination, the talented, excellent person who finishes what he or she starts and submits it on time? Isn't that a nice ideal to strive for and to make a consistent reality?

I also want to point out that having a problem with lateness is not as clear and easy as it sounds. I had a coaching client, a senior in high school, and her mother hired me because she was worried about what would happen to her daughter when she went to the Ivy League college that she had been accepted to the following Fall. She did okay in high school – well enough to get accepted to an Ivy League school – but she was often late in turning her assignments or waiting till the last minute to study for exams.

Her mother was convinced her daughter had a lateness problem.

In our several once a week coaching session, we discussed various time management concepts and principles. Her daughter also shared with me about her family life. What I learned was that her turning homework in late as well as studying at the last minute for her tests was tied to her perfectionism issues. The procrastination that she was evidencing, and the lateness problem that she was labeled as having, were covering up her fear of disappointing her parents, her teacher, or herself. To reduce, minimize, or eliminate her delaying or lateness challenges, she needed to work on building up her self-esteem as well as recognizing, and overcoming, her perfectionism challenges.

So, if you or someone you know has a lateness challenge, try to look at the underlying causes. In understanding those causes, and what to do to rectify each one, the solution will be found. Just telling someone to start being on time, whether it is being on time at work, or in turning in required projects isn't enough. You have to let them know there will be consequences if this behavior continues.

Devaluing yourself or your goal

If you devalue yourself or what it is that you need to finish, it will unfortunately be too easy to put the project aside as you tell yourself, "Who cares anyway?" or "Am I really that important that this matters?"

Sometimes it takes just the right amount of self-love and self-esteem to keep yourself on track till you finish what you started whether it's something as relatively minor like baking a cake, or learning how to use new software, or something a lot more complex, like figuring out what major to take in college, and completing all the necessary coursework to graduate.

If you devalue what you must finish, you might think that no one really cares, or it will not make that much of an impact, if you finish anyway, so why bother? Does your niece really care whether her birthday card arrives right before, or on, her birthday? Does it make that much difference whether your desk is neat and organized before you have the next review by your supervisor?

Overvaluing yourself or your goal

If you have too inflated an opinion of yourself, or you exaggerate the importance of what you must do, you might get "shut down" because all the fears I mentioned in the beginning of this chapter kick in. Does your dissertation really have to be the most amazing piece of research ever written or is it just an exercise that you need to go through to get the doctorate that you want to complete? There are exceptions to every rule. How fortunate we all are that Emile Durkheim made his dissertation, *The Division of Labor in Society,* the magnum opus that he did. What a contribution he made to sociology for all time. You just might be the next Durkheim, or Einstein, but if putting yourself in such a category makes it even harder for you to function, and do your best, then it might be time to reevaluate how you view yourself, so it is more realistic without being self-deprecating or putting yourself down.

Adjusting how you value what it is you are putting off will probably help you finish. The play you are writing may not be as good as Shakespeare or Tennessee Williams, but if you finish it and get it produced, it will be your play and it might even be a good or excellent play.

The trip you are planning with your family for next summer may not be the vacation of a lifetime, or a dream trip, but if you make the airline reservations, and commit to a resort or destination that everyone wants to visit, you are more likely to be creating positive family memories than if you put things off till the last minute and either end up not going anywhere or are stuck with less desirable options because everything else is sold out.

Failing to plan for, or allow, interruptions

Another reason for failing to finish is that you are so unprepared for interruptions that when one or more occur, you get thrown by it. If you put something aside, because you absolutely have to address another more pressing professional or personal concern, you get into the "out of sight, out of mind" situation, noted before, rather than letting the interrupt happen and, once it is addressed, getting right back to this concern.

One way to deal better with interruptions so that it is less likely to derail you is to reframe interruptions as necessary and predictable rather than unforeseen occurrences that make it harder for you to stay in control of your own priorities.

Being too inconsistent in your effort

Finally, most of us will agree that having a routine can make it easier to stick to something until it is done. Although some may find they can still get a lot done even if they work on this a little bit, and that a little bit, moving each project along, even if you do that, there is a rhythm to that plan so that it is actually more consistent than it sounds. Ideally, you will start, and keep going, till something is done. But if you can only work on something a little bit, try to put in some time every day, every week, or over the weekend.

Consistency is a concept that has a different meaning for each of us. One person's routine may be another person's boredom. What is key is to know how much time and effort you are allocating to a task, project, or concern. If you are not getting the result you want, you may have to switch it up. I am reminded of that adage, "Slow and steady wins the race."

EXERCISES

1. Look over the behaviors, beliefs, and bad habits named and discussed in this chapter. Pick the #1-time waster that you are dealing with when it comes to preventing you from finishing everything you start. Write down that time waster here.

   ____

   What do you plan to do to try to turn around this tendency? Write down your plan here:

   ____

   ____

   How will you know that you have improved in this regard?

   ____

   Write down the date 2 weeks from today.

   ____

   That is the day you will check up on yourself to see if you have made progress dealing with this time waster.

2. Think about someone you know who does finish everything he or she starts and turns things in on time. What are some of the behavior traits that you notice about him or her that might be exemplary for you? Is there a consistency to when he or she arrives at work? How often, if ever, does he or

she get personal calls during the work day? How often does he or she check his or her smartphone for text messages or e-mails?

3. Write down a brief description of at least one project or task that you have not finished that you want to complete.

____

What is stopping you from completing it?

____

What are you going to do about that challenge?

____

In Chapter 5 we will discuss why interim deadlines are useful, not just one far away deadline. But for now, write down a deadline that you think you can realistically meet to finish this project.

____

What do you need to do to meet that deadline?

____

____

CHAPTER 3

Having Too Much to Do at Once

There are eight key reasons people give for failing to finish something. By far the #1 reason for leaving a task or project unfinished is having too much to do. Thirty percent (30.54%) of the 203 men and women I surveyed picked that reason. What is even more telling is that this reason crosses international borders: for the 153 Americans, "I have too much to do" was the top reason for twenty-eight percent (28.10%) as well as for the 47 Indians in Asia. For them, thirty-eight percent (38.30%), even more than the overall, chose that reason.

I'm a time management expert and sometimes I find myself having too much to do. A few years ago, this problem got so bad I made a "to do list" and guess how many things were on it? Would you believe 47? Talk about having too much to do at once!

If most of us list everything we have to do at any given moment, many of us will come up with a list of ten, maybe 20 tasks or projects, for work, school, or personal reasons.

But that's where the syndrome of leaving things undone comes in. It's virtually impossible to do ten or 20 things at once. You have to decide what's most important and prioritize.

This is a skill that I will go into in greater detail in Chapter 7, "Taking Control: Goal Setting and Prioritizing." For now, just be aware that the way to finish everything you start is to have a clear plan of what you need to do now and what you can put off until later.

In addition to learning to do one thing at a time or, if you do a couple of things simultaneously, to at least practice selective attention. That means when you are doing one thing, that thing takes all your focus. Then you can switch to something else, and then that concern gets your concentration. But you are not literally going back and forth between the projects.

Some suggest that you always finish one project before you are going on to the next one. In an ideal world, we would all do that. I would love to say that I do that. Sometimes I do because it is a task that is self-contained and could be done at one sitting. Creating a syllabus for a course, for example, is something that I can usually do in one sitting, although that time span might be anywhere from two to six hours, depending upon whether it is a syllabus from scratch or the revision of a tried-and-true syllabus that is just being updated with new dates and possibly some new information or references.

But extensive and intricate projects may take many hours. For most us, that is where the unfinished syndrome kicks in. Whether it is doing a long-term project that is going to take days, weeks, or months, for business, or reorganizing the closets, or cleaning out the garage, at home, how many of those kinds of more complex and time-consuming projects can you handle at once?

The "I have too much to do at once" obstacle to finishing everything you start is also tied to an inability to say "no." Chapter 9 will help you with this. In "Learning to Say 'No,'' you will begin to master the art of turning someone down without offending that person. Anyone can say an abrupt "no," but saying "no" so that you are still high on someone's list, whether it's at work or in your personal life. That's an art and a skill that fortunately it is possible to master.

What does it mean when someone states, "I have too much to do?" It means that there are too many competing priorities and that individual is having a tough time deciding what to do now, next, or even never. I do not want to steal the thunder of the all-important chapter on goal setting and prioritizing in the next part so for now, let me just reassure you that you can do what you need to do. You can! Here are some affirmations that relate to that concept which I firmly believe in:

I can do all I have to do right now.

I am handling whatever I need to do.

I am finishing what I am working on now.

I am making good choices about what I should be doing right now.

Whatever I am working on now is getting my full attention.

When is the last time you said to someone, "I have too much to do?" or that someone said that to you?

Maybe they said it in another way, "I'm too busy!"

When did being busy become a bad thing? When someone complains to me, "I'm too busy!" I like to reply by asking, "But are you 'good' busy?"

I think I have always enjoyed being busy. Being idle has been boring to me. But that does not mean I don't take time out to smell the roses. I just think being busy has been getting a negative connotation lately. I have been involved in time mangement and productivity training and writing long enough to remember the focus in the 1980s on the workaholic. That was the concept and the word that so many were addressing. I recall the key point of the research into workaholism is that workaholics have a hard time starting, and stopping, so they work all the time. They are not as productive as those who pace themselves because workaholics increase the likelihood that they will suffer from burnout and stop working on a specific project, or even at a certain job, all together. That is the opposite of productive.

Today we know that it is possible to be busy, and to have many demands on your time, but if you practice the principles of time management that you are learning, or reinforcing, in this book, you are more likely to finish whatever you start. You may have to learn to order or reorder the way in which you go about doing what it is that you need to do, but you can — and will — get it all done, and then some. I know these principles work because I apply these principles each day and to the many projects — professional and personal — that I must do.

So please finish up this chapter, before the exercises, by restating this as a mantra: "I am making a choice about what I am doing now."

In the next chapter, we examine procrastination, the second most frequent cause of failing to finish. However, it is a very distant second to "I have too much to do at once" coming in at just 8.37% compared to the 30.54% for the "too much at once syndrome."

EXERCISES

1. Do you feel that "I have too much to do at once?" If you answered "yes," make a list of all the things you must do —want to do —now. Make that list as long and as extensive as possible. Avoid censoring yourself or ranking what you must do in importance. We will return to this list when we address prioritizing in Chapter 7.

   What I need to do now

   1. ______________________________
   2. ______________________________
   3. ______________________________
   4. ______________________________
   5. ______________________________
   6. ______________________________
   7. ______________________________
   8. ______________________________
   9. ______________________________

10. ______________________________

11. ______________________________

12. ______________________________

13. ______________________________

14. ______________________________

15. ______________________________

16. ______________________________

17. ______________________________

18. ______________________________

19. ______________________________

20. ______________________________

21. ______________________________

22. ______________________________

23. ______________________________

24. ______________________________

25. ______________________________

26. ______________________________

27. ______________________________

28. ______________________________

29. ______________________________

30. ______________________________

31. ______________________________

32. ______________________________

33. ______________________________

34. ______________________________

35. ______________________________

36. ______________________________

37. ______________________________

38. ______________________________

39. ______________________________

40. ______________________________

41. ______________________________

42. ______________________________

43. ______________________________

44. ______________________________

45. ______________________________

46. ______________________________

47. ______________________________

48. ______________________________

49. ______________________________

50. ______________________________

2. Now go back to that list. Circle or highlight the top three items that you must do.

   Must do's:

   1. ________________

   2. ________________

   3. ________________

Now look over the complete list of things to do and list the three things you want to do:

1. ___________________________

2. ___________________________

3. ___________________________

For now, the issue is not whether your musts or wants match up. But it may be eye-opening to see if that is true. Also, even though this book is geared toward making sure you get all your "musts" done, since that is usually what you must do for work, business, or for school, the "wants" that you have unfinished are still key to address as well.

3. Think back to a time when you did only one thing at a time, if you ever were in that position. When was that?

   ____

   ____

   What did it feel like to be focused on just one thing?

   ____

   What was the outcome?

   ____

   ____

CHAPTER 4

Dealing with Procrastination

We previously established that my philosophy is that procrastination is also information. So, let's explore that concept further since procrastination is the #2 reason that a task or project is unfinished.

What information might procrastination be providing for you? Think of an unfinished project that you would love to complete. Here is a list of just some of the tasks, projects, or even relationship concerns that the 205 that I surveyed shared that they left unfinished:

- "Completing my work or task on the very same day it was given to me"
- "Write a novel"
- "Not get time for my gym"
- "Writing a report of my industrial field visit"
- "My dream project"
- "I never did my homework"
- "Complete my degree"
- "My aim to study and achieve competitive exam"
- "Cleaning my house"
- "Downsizing my house"
- "Getting married"
- "Making a vision video for the organization"
- "Sorting family photos"
- "Saving money"
- "Graduating from college"
- "Losing 10 pounds"

- "Getting a job"
- "Finishing my new house project"
- "Decluttering my home"
- "Spending more time with grandson"

What is yours? Write it down here:

____

Now we are going to address why you might be procrastinating about finishing that task, project, or relationship goal.

First, let's review what I see as the definition of procrastination: putting off something that you should or want to do. I used to add in that it was putting off something unpleasant by doing something else, something more positive and fun. But I must revise that definition because sometimes the thing you are procrastinating about is more fun than the substitute activity.

So why would someone procrastinate if he or she is putting off doing something that he or she wants to do? What is done instead may be less pleasant. Instead of finishing up a report that you know will help you advance in your career, you make cold calls that are very demanding and stressful. Taking a web development course that you have been procrastinating about taking might even empower you to do your own website giving you more creative control and even saving you money.

In Chapter 2 we looked at 22-time wasters and bad habits that can stop you from finishing one or more tasks or projects that you want to — must — do. So many of those time wasters or bad habits are possible reasons behind your procrastination. If you have a fear of failure, you will delay finishing a project, so you do not have to deal with the potential negative feedback that you fear. If you fear success, procrastination delays that scenario from happening.

Perfectionism is behind procrastination for some; fearing that your effort will come up short, you delay and delay to avoid having to face your own imperfections. Poor pacing and poor planning may be behind your procrastination, but it might be your body or mind forcing you to take a break. If you have been at the computer for eight hours straight, and your eyes are starting to glaze over, taking a walk, or a nap, or calling it a day may be positive actions, not signs of procrastination.

Emotional turmoil can cause procrastination because if you are dealing with a lot of stress or personal angst in your life, it could be hard to concentrate on certain tights of tasks. Your emotions may be requiring you to take a break, and deal with your issues, before returning to the project at hand. So, in that case, your procrastination has a reason behind it. It is not delay for the sake of delay or because of bad work habits.

Ditto for working under pressure backfiring on you. As noted before, procrastination may be information. If you are under severe pressure on a project, procrastination may be your mind and body's way of getting what you need.

I want to share an example from my own life in this regard. For the first time in my entire college teaching career, I taught a summer course this year. It was a three-week intensive. I had the challenge of teaching 16 weeks of Soc 203 – Criminology – in just 3 weeks. (I always referred to it as a 3-week intensive course. However, the students liked to say that it was just 11 days.)

I am pleased to report that it turned out quite well. In addition to covering the entire textbook, as well as having five quizzes, a required presentation, and a fieldwork assignment, we had one guest speaker and two field trips to a work-release correctional facility nearby and two alternatives to incarceration programs at a court.

Just before the end of the course, however, on a very hot day, since my ride back to Connecticut would not be available for many hours, rather than go to my office to work, I went to the movies. I saw a documentary about the Supreme Court Justice, Ruth Bader Ginsberg called RBG.

Those couple of hours at the movie theater was just what the doctor ordered, as they say. I went by myself since I did not want to socialize with anyone else. After another intense day of teaching – the summer course goes from 9 a.m. till 12:45 P.M., almost 4 hours – I just wanted to see a movie and relax.

Some might call it procrastinating. I prefer to see it as a positive way of taking care of myself.

The only problem with taking time off to do something that you need to do – when it turns into procrastination – is when you cannot switch gears and get back to your required tasks in a timely fashion.

When the break or time off gets out of hand, you need to do something about the situation before you fall so far behind in your work, or personal commitments, that you start getting yelled at. So here are some tips for dealing with procrastination if it has become a time waster and problem for you:

1 Try the reward system.

For me, going to the movie was my reward for the hard work I was doing teaching that intensive course. What will you choose to reward yourself with, so you can control taking a break before it becomes too frequent or systemic? Make sure you make the reward something that you enjoy doing so it is a true motivator.

Write down what you are procrastinating about here:

I am procrastinating about

____

Now write down your reward.

If I do what I need to do — must do — this is how I will reward myself.

____

2 Allow for delays.

Instead of fighting the tendency to procrastinate, allow for delays.

Like the reward system, plan how you will build one or more delays into your day, or even your week. I am reminded of what dentists used to do when I was growing up. My father was a dentist. He always took Thursdays off. Most dentists used that time to relax or possibly even play golf. My father volunteered at the local VA (Veterans Administration) hospital. For him, it was a break from his routine of working on civilian patients. That day, or delay, enabled him to return refreshed to his regular practice.

Use the space below to plan out your delays.
I will take a break – allow for a delay – at

______________ hour

or

______________ day

3 Try what I called *creative procrastination* in my book, *Creative Time Management for the New Millennium.*

Creative procrastination is a very powerful tool. If you do it effectively, you can find yourself more productive than ever before, finishing more and more projects. If you use it unwisely or in the wrong way, you can find yourself with many – far too many – projects that are unfinished, the exact opposite of what we are trying to achieve with this book.

Here is the key part of creative procrastination that will help you to use it in the service of finishing things, not creating more unfinished tasks or projects. Use creative procrastination to get something finished. What I mean by that is this: You must write a report. You are blocked on the introduction. Instead of putting down the report, and going on to another task, you find something within the report that you can do, such as the bibliography, or doing original research, or reviewing what you wrote the day before.

So, you use the concept of creative procrastination to move a specific project along till that project is done.

It is a bit like the concept of breaking a large task down into more manageable smaller tasks, one of the time mangement key principles. But instead of breaking down the task into smaller steps, this is a matter of moving around from task to task within a specific activity that you need to do, whether it's clean your office or finish up that report, tackling another part of the required task or project, making a commitment to yourself to keep going till that task is done, finished!

4 Make whatever you are procrastinating about the very first activity that you tackle first thing in the morning, or when you first get to the office.

Instead of checking e-mails or going on the Internet and getting distracted by reading articles or doing lots of necessary tasks but activities unrelated to the project you want to finish, make that the task you do as you begin your day. Most people are freshest in the morning, especially if they are what is called a "morning" person. But even if you are not a morning person, if you make that key project that you want to finish the first thing you do that day, you can at least zone in on it before all the many disparate demands on your time pull you in a million directions.

5 Find a great place to stop for the day.

If you end whatever you are trying to finish at a good point, it will be that much easier to pick right up again when you can get back to it. That could help you avoid procrastinating about finishing it by going on to other tasks or projects.

What is a good place to stop? This will depend on everyone. For me, when I am writing a book, I prefer to stop for the day at the end of a chapter. That's a nice solid finishing point for me. It makes it easy to start the next day at the next chapter, whether I am writing the book in order or out of order.

Some prefer to stop their work during it, so they can pick it up again more easily for them.

There is no right or wrong way for that but do figure out what works best for you.

6 Partner with someone.

If you are putting something off, perhaps partnering with someone about it will help you to stop delaying. Whether it is someone that you just talk to about what you are procrastinating about, or someone that you could work with on a project or task so together you tackle it, sometimes having someone else involved can propel you out of the block that you are having from "doing."

EXERCISES

1. What are you procrastinating about right now? Pick out at least one thing you are putting off that you would like to be doing.

   ____

Review the six suggested ways of dealing with procrastination as it relates to this one thing you are procrastinating about. How will you overcome procrastinating about it using one or more of those ways? Use the worksheet below to work out a plan.

Overcoming procrastination tactic #1

____

Overcoming procrastination tactic #2

____

Overcoming procrastination tactic #3

____

2. Here are some words that many associate with procrastination. Circle the ones that you think apply to your procrastination.

- lazy
- bored
- disorganized
- overwhelmed
- busy
- creative procrastination
- procrastination as information
- excellent time manager
- self-loving
- self-nurturing
- poor planning
- poor pacing
- positive self-talk
- chronically late
- perfectionist
- fear of failure
- fear of success
- poor time manager
- excellent planning
- commendable pacing
- allowing for delays
- workaholic
- stressed out
- stress-free
- relaxed
- reward system

Now go back and look at how many concepts you circled that are negative. How many are positive?

Negative terms I checked off related to procrastination and me

____

Positive terms I checked off related to procrastination and me

____

How will you work on converting the negative terms about yourself related to procrastination to positive ones?

____

____

____

CHAPTER 5

Rethinking Deadlines

In Chapter 2 we briefly explored the consequences of having an unrealistic deadline. Let's look at the word: deadline. It is made up of two words: dead + line.

Line is easy enough to relate to. There is a line that you should not cross. Usually the line is the date that has been set to complete something and turn it in.

But what about this first part of the word? Dead? Where does that come from?

No one likes to think about death and certainly death is a very negative image if you associate it with your task or project.

Where does the term deadline come from? I associate it with the deadline for a newspaper story. If something happens, the story usually had to be filed by the time the paper went to press. Consulting the online version of the 90-year-old *Oxford English Dictionary (OED),* the definition of deadline is, "A line that does not move or run."

The OED lists three different origins of the word. The first is military, dating back to 1864 as noted by the *Congressional Record* on January 12, 1876, that a "dead line: was the line "beyond which the prisoners are not allowed to pass." Another military reference from 1868 as noted in the OED: "Seventeen feet from the inner stockade was the 'dead-line', over which no man could pass and live.'

In addition to several military references to a deadline in that context is the context in printing: "A guide-line marked on the bed of a printing-press."

Finally, OED has a third connotation for the word *deadline*: "a time by which material has to be ready for inclusion in a particular issue of a publication."

I am here to tell you that if you want to finish everything

you start — at least those things that you selectively decide you want to finish — you need to embrace deadlines as a positive thing, rather than something to be dreaded.

For starters, consider if you must change your attitude toward deadlines by taking this self-quiz.

SELF-QUIZ

How Do You Feel About Deadlines?

Answer the questions below with a yes, no, sometimes, or often response. This self-quiz is for your own introspection so be as open and honest as possible.

1. When I hear the word "deadline" I get angry.
   Yes ☐ No ☐ Sometimes ☐ Often ☐

2. I am neutral toward deadlines.
   Yes ☐ No ☐ Sometimes ☐ Often ☐

3. If a project I am working on does not have a deadline, I will impose one on it myself.
   Yes ☐ No ☐ Sometimes ☐ Often ☐

4. I consider having a deadline being told what to do.
   Yes ☐ No ☐ Sometimes ☐ Often ☐

5. If I were the boss, I would eliminate deadlines.
   Yes ☐ No ☐ Sometimes ☐ Often ☐

6. Looking back on when I have been most productive, it was tied to meeting or beating a deadline.
   Yes ☐ No ☐ Sometimes ☐ Often ☐

7. If I am working on a complex project, even if there is one final deadline, I will create interim deadlines to keep myself (and/or my team) on track.
   Yes ☐ No ☐ Sometimes ☐ Often ☐

8. I have a daily, weekly, and/or annual appointment book or planner where I record the key deadlines I need to consider.
   Yes ☐ No ☐ Sometimes ☐ Often ☐

9. I consider a deadline a useful way to prioritize my commitments and time so I am more likely to get my priority projects done.
   Yes ☐ No ☐ Sometimes ☐ Often ☐

10. In the last year, I have had to renegotiate a deadline at least once.
    Yes ☐ No ☐ Sometimes ☐ Often ☐

11. I like a deadline because it helps me to plan and stay on track.
    Yes ☐ No ☐ Sometimes ☐ Often ☐

Now review your responses. If you answered to number one, "When I hear the word 'deadline' I get angry," you have a deadline challenge that may be holding you back from finishing tasks or projects in as timely a way as possible. Fortunately, recognizing this is your real feeling about deadlines will help you to reframe your attitude so you have a more neutral attitude, as reflected in your answer to question 2 or in your answer to the last question, number 11, "I like a deadline because it helps me to plan and stay on track."

Hopefully your answer to that is either a yes, sometimes or often.

Look over the rest of the questions and your answers. Which answers reflect a negative attitude toward deadlines? Which answers show you have a positive attitude, but that it is inconsistent?

Reframing how you view deadlines may just be the attitude makeover that you need to finish more of the tasks or projects that you want to, or need to, complete.

Several respondents in my snowball sample finishing survey stated that if she or he failed to finish something the reason was "The task or project didn't have a deadline; it is an open-ended situation."

If someone says to you, "Get that to me when you're finished," and that person fails to give you a deadline, give yourself one!

If you do not have a deadline for an important task or project, you need to create one for yourself.

If you have a deadline, is it one big deadline, a week, a month, or even a year down the road, or are there shorter, interim deadlines which will make it easier for you to organize yourself and whatever it is that you need to do?

The first way that deadlines will be helpful to you is by having one.

Having just one deadline, however, is often not enough, especially for longer, more complicated projects. You might need multiple deadlines.

The second biggest mistake that is made when it comes to deadlines is that too often deadlines are unrealistic. We discussed this in regard to software projects that are so ridiculously underestimated that they're sometimes referred to as the Death March. The problem does not just happen with software development projects, but with many tasks and projects. These can range from planning an event to writing an article, from preparing a dinner party for eight to researching and writing a term paper.

Deadlines are usually helpful, even for shorter or simpler tasks, such as "I will get to the bank by two o'clock," if you are not doing all your banking on phone or online, or "I will return those phone calls by five."

But for more complicated projects, deadlines are crucial. As noted before, interim deadlines are useful, not just one deadline.

The key is to be realistic. I discussed how too often you may be tempted to agree to an unrealistic deadline because you fear someone else will get the assignment if you confess how long something will really take, but unfortunately you are setting yourself up for a very difficult situation. Rather than motivate you to get the job done, it may it harder for you to finish in not just a timely manner but by doing your best work. Rushing might sabotage your goal of doing praiseworthy work. So, you do want to finish, and finish in a timely fashion, but you want to allot a realistic amount of time to the job at hand.

There is also the other side of the coin, however. If you ask for too much time, even if it is granted, the deadline may be so far away that you put off getting to that project or you are tempted to complete other jobs ahead of that one.

Deadlines are somewhat like *Goldilocks and the Three Bears*, that classic fairy tale. Not too far away, not too near, it needs to be just right! The good news about imposing deadlines on yourself is that you get to have more control over projects and situations.

Breaking Bigger Tasks Up into Smaller More Manageable Ones

Tied to the concept of creating a realistic deadline that helps to move a project along to completion is the time management idea of breaking big tasks up into more manageable one. That is also tied to the benefits of interim deadlines, rather than one big deadline that looms far in the distance.

What project do you want to finish that might benefit from

breaking it down into more manageable tasks?

Once you break that larger project down into more manageable tasks, now give each of those tasks a deadline, within the overall deadline for the entire project.

For a book, especially if it is a nonfiction book, it is a logical breakdown of "writing a book" into writing each chapter. The same principle of working on a chapter at a time could hold for a novel although it may be much more intricate and unique to each book since some novelists go back and forth in time and some may even prefer to write the ending before the beginning.

This concept of breaking complicated tasks into more manageable ones, with interim deadlines for each other tasks, can be applied to all the work and personal projects that you have. It makes everything, from doing the inviting, shopping, and cooking for a dinner party for eight to planning a wedding and honeymoon, or a family vacation, something that is less unwieldy with all the various pieces of the puzzle to get completed.

In Part 2, "Cures" that follows, we will examine more ways to cure yourself of failing to finish everything you start.

In summary, deadlines can be useful tools in your quest to finish everything you start!

EXERCISES

1. Make a list of the top 3 projects that you must do that are unfinished. Do you have a deadline for any or all these projects? If you do, write it down. If you do not, create one now. Make sure you consider how realistic the deadline is for each project. Also, if you have only one deadline, add in at least one, maybe even more, interim deadlines, depending upon how complex or detailed the project at hand is.

   Unfinished Project/Task to Do #1

   ____

Final deadline for completion:

____

Interim deadline #1:

____

Interim deadline #2:

____

In addition to writing down the interim deadlines, note what you will accomplish by each interim deadline. This is a version of the time management principle of breaking a large task into smaller, more manageable ones.

Unfinished Project/Task to Do #2

____

Final deadline for completion:

____

Interim deadline #1:

____

Interim deadline #2:

____

Unfinished Project/Task to Do #3

____

Final deadline for completion:

____

Interim deadline #1:

____

Interim deadline #2:

____

3. Consider your attitude toward deadlines. Do you love 'em, hate 'em, are you indifferent? If deadlines are not for you, especially if you do the kind of work, or live the kind of life, that you do not need deadlines, that's fine. What will you do instead to keep yourself on track? Or maybe you do use dates to monitor your progress, but you do not call it a deadline? Use the space below to consider how you track what you need to do, and when it needs to be accomplished, as a way of helping yourself to finish more often and within the time frame that you wish.

PART 2: CURES

CHAPTER 6

Using F-I-N-I-S-H

Having an acronym to remind you about the short cuts to finish could be a helpful tool to keep you on track. I am, therefore, pleased to share the acronym that I created that helps me.

F = Focus on one priority task.

I = Ignore interruptions or distractions.

N = Now is the time, not later or tomorrow.

I = Initiate and innovate so you keep going.

S = Stay the course however tough it gets.

H = Hail finishing by celebrating your accomplishment.

Let's explore each of these concepts in greater detail.

F = Focus on one priority task.

Getting distracted and doing too many things at once, as we have seen, leads to many unfinished tasks. It's one of the biggest obstacles to finishing anything. Pick one priority project and stick with it!

I = Ignore interruptions or distractions.

Interruptions will happen, and you must take care of crises at work or personal responsibilities. But as soon as you have dealt with the interruption, get back to the project at hand. It's those self-made interruptions you need to take control of. Do you really need to stop and read your emails now?

N = Now is the time, not later or tomorrow.

Procrastination, or putting something off for later, tomorrow, or even weeks or months down the road, is a big impediment to getting things done. So, make a commitment that this priority task is going to be your focus now, not later, not even tomorrow.

I = Initiate and innovate so you keep going.

Starting can be a challenge, especially if it's something you have been trying to finish but you keep putting it off, again and again. But once you initiate, you can keep going, and that is what you need to do. If you are distracted or finding yourself wandering away from this priority concern, be innovative in how you can keep yourself on track. There are timers you can buy, or you can use your smartphone, to set an alarm if you can keep focused for an hour or two or more. Knowing that you are keeping on track and, when you hear that alarm go off, rewarding yourself with that sound that you have been working toward a goal can be a way to push yourself forward.

S = Stay the course however tough it gets.

It's said that Thomas Edison made 1,000 attempts before he was able to successfully invent the light bulb. So whatever you are working on probably will not have the history-making and lifestyle-changing impact of the invention of the light bulb, but it could make all the difference in your career or even your personal life. So, remind yourself how Edison kept at it and follow his lead.

H = Hail finishing by celebrating your accomplishment.

When you do finish, pat yourself on the back. Whether your boss or coworkers applaud you, clap for yourself. Reward yourself with something tangible or even ask a friend, romantic partner, or family member to go out and celebrate with you. You have finished something and if completing things is a challenge for you, then you especially deserve to make it a big deal that you have achieved that goal. The more positive you make the act of finishing, the more you conquer whatever fears, time wasters, or bad habits have held you back, the more likely finishing will get easier and easier until it is no longer the challenge it has become.

Before we go on to the next chapter, where we will address goal setting and prioritizing, let's look at two key concepts that will help you to finish what you start.

The first is finding hidden time and the second is getting on top of how you are spending your time. If you have not done it before, or if you are not currently doing it, keeping a time log can help you see where your time is going.

Finding and Making the Most of Hidden Time

We're all busy, but if you put our mind to it, you might be able to carve out what I call "hidden" time each workday, evening, or weekend. What is hidden time? It's time that you previously wasted because you were less cognizant of the passage of time or, if you commute to work, for example, you did not consider how to best make use of those minutes or hours on the train, bus, airplane, or in your car that might help you to finish what you started.

Even if you carry a smartphone, consider throwing a small notebook into your pocketbook, suitcase, or tote so you can jot down thoughts related to whatever tasks you are working on, or even writing drafts of important e-mails that you prefer to work on rather than dash off.

Hidden time might include the time you spend in the office of a professional, such as a dentist or a doctor, waiting for your appointment. Unless you have a reason to read the magazines in the waiting room, if you brought along a book to read, or the hard copy of the project that you are working on, those minutes in the waiting room suddenly become a way to better utilize your hidden time.

Sometimes you are unaware of just what you are doing with your time on an hourly, daily, or weekly basis. If this is not the first time management-related book that you have read, then you know about keeping a time log and how valuable a tool such a log could be. If you have a detailed appointment book, you can just use it to create a time log to help you see where you have your hidden time. You could use your actual appointment book or photocopy a couple of pages, so you keep the appointments blocked out in your book clear from the more detailed log that you are now keeping.

How Do You Currently Handle Your Time?

Here is a sample of a time log that you can use to record how you are currently handling your time. (If you have an appointment book, and it is detailed enough, you might use that for your time log recoding. There is also a sample appointment log in the Appendix that you might apply to creating your time log.)

You could either write directly on this page or photocopy it, so you can keep several days of time logs to monitor where your time is currently going. If you wake up at 7, just jump down to the 7 A.M. entry on the log. If you wake up at 5, start there.

Time Logs

DAILY TIME LOG 1

TODAY'S DATE: ________________

DAY OF THE WEEK: ___________

TYPE OF DAY: ________________ (Work? School? Leisure?)

TIME	ACTIVITY
______	*Wake Up*
______	______
______	______
______	______
______	______
______	______
______	______
______	______
______	______
______	______
______	______
______	______
______	______
______	______
______	______
______	______

Conclude your day with the time you go to sleep:

______ ______

COMMENTS (Try to notice if there are any times when you are especially alert, or particularly tired, as well as any peaks of efficiency, periods of heightened concentration, and times when you pay better attention to details. At what times are you better or worse at working with people—both in person and over the phone?)

______

______

______

____

____

DAILY TIME LOG 2

TODAY'S DATE: __________________

DAY OF THE WEEK: ____________

TYPE OF DAY: __________________ (Work? School? Leisure?)

TIME	ACTIVITY
________	*Wake Up*
________	______________________________
________	______________________________
________	______________________________
________	______________________________
________	______________________________
________	______________________________
________	______________________________
________	______________________________
________	______________________________
________	______________________________
________	______________________________
________	______________________________
________	______________________________
________	______________________________
________	______________________________

Conclude your day with the time you go to sleep:

_______ ____________________________________

COMMENTS (Try to notice if there are any times when you are especially alert, or particularly tired, as well as any peaks of efficiency, periods of heightened concentration, and times when you pay better attention to details. At what times are you better or worse at working with people—both in person and over the phone?)

____

____

____

____

____

Put aside your time log or logs for now. You will return to reviewing your logs in the next chapter.

Here are some suggestions about what to do with the hidden time that you find, whether it is during your commuting time, in the evenings, during your lunch hour at work, or on the weekends:

1. Have a plan for how you will make better use of your hidden time.
2. Bring along a hand-held computer, iPad, or smartphone that you can use to take notes, do work, or even relax and watch a video, TV program, or listen to music.
3. Exercise during your hidden time.

4. Meditate.
5. Daydream.
6. Brainstorm with one or more co-workers, by phone, Skype, or in person.
7. Socialize.
8. Nap (if there is a safe way to do this and/or you will not be seen as lazy or ignoring your duties. Some progressive companies have nap rooms or even lounge chairs in the bathroom where it is acceptable to take a short nap.)
9. Reconsider your short- and long-term goals,
10. Have stationary, note cards, or commercial cards that you fill out and send.
11. Have a physical book or read electronically or listen to an audiobook.
12. Do a chore or errand that needs to be done so you have a bigger block of time after work or in your leisure time.
13. Consider one thing that you have unfinished. Write down at least 3 reasons why finishing will be beneficial to you professionally or personally.

EXERCISES

1. Apply F-I-N-I-S-H to an unfinished task or project.

   The F is the project that you are Focusing on. Write it down.

   ____

   How will you stop yourself from being I (interrupted)?

Interruption-free plan

____

Will you promise yourself to focus on this project or task N (now) and not put it off? Yes ____ No _____

What will you I (initiate) or innovate to help yourself finish this project?

____

Are you **S** (staying the course) on this project?

Yes____ No ____

If you checked off "no, please go back to the first letters to get yourself back on track.

Or, if necessary, go back to Chapter 2 and review the 22 beliefs, behaviors, or bad habits that could be holding you back, or reread Chapter 4, Dealing with Procrastination."

Finally, as soon as you finish this project —and if it is a complex project, you should be breaking it down into more manageable steps, as discussed in greater detail in Chapter 5, "Rethinking Deadlines." Once you F-I-N-I-S-H —whether it is an entire project or a piece of a bigger undertaking —do something to celebrate your accomplishment! Reinforce the act of finishing!

Look over the six (6) letters in the F-I-N-I-S-H acronym. Find the one letter or principle that is most challenging for you and that might be the strongest reason behind your tendency to delay, quit, or fail to finish. Write down that letter and the concept that goes with it.

____

How will you work on turning around this tendency?

____

Once you feel you have improved that letter/issue in the F-I-N-I-S-H acronym, go on to the next letter or issue that is challenging you until you have gone through all six letters, strengthening your finishing muscle.

CHAPTER 7

Taking Control: Goal Setting and Prioritizing

I can hear some of you thinking or saying this out loud, "No, not goal setting and prioritizing again! Enough about setting goals and prioritizing. Tell me something I do not already know!"

If you've read one or more books on time management, or attended a workshop, or even done an online training or taken a webinar, goal setting and prioritizing are basic concepts that you will learn. Even if you are familiar with these key productivity ideas, it is worth reviewing the basics as well as revisiting these concepts considering the world that you find yourself working and living in right now. It is a much more frenzied world practically everywhere on the globe. You might be able to find a remote location without cell phone service or lots of distractions, but it is getting harder and harder to do that.

Setting a Goal Will Help You Decide What to Tackle First

One of my favorite habits of *The 7 Habits of Highly Successful People*, Dr. Stephen Covey's classic nonfiction self-help book, is Habit 2, "Begin with the End in Mind." This concept is part of the very insightful discussion related to Habit 2 in which Covey explains that "*all things are created twice*. There's a mental or first creation, and a physical or second creation to all things." (The italics for emphasis is based on the style in the 1989 edition of Covey's book.)

Covey goes on to explain that the two creations in Habit 2 is founded on the principle of personal leadership. According to that principle, the first creation is leadership. The second creation is management. He goes on to explain the difference between leadership and management. If you are in the jungle, it is the leader who "climbs the tallest tree, surveys the entire situation, and yells, 'Wrong jungle!'"

This relates to the reason goal setting is so pivotal to selectively finishing everything you start. You need to have short- and long-term goals so that you can make the judgment call about what you should be finishing now, next week, next month, or in five years.

Goals at work and in your personal life help you to know what you want to achieve. Once you have a clearer vision of just what you want to accomplish you can put the time and energy into making it happen.

But goals do not have to be stagnant. Some flexibility is in order especially if those adjustments are because of a change in circumstances, or even your values, rather than allowing one of the 22-time wasters or bad habits we explored in Chapter 2 as the reason a goal, or task or project, is being delayed or abandoned.

Goals help you to "stay the course" and to react with clarity and determination to challenges and opportunities rather than faltering or wondering what to do in each situation.

Today's goal for me is to continue writing *How to Finish Everything You Start* until the book is done. No ambiguity there. I woke up and quickly checked e-mails, book sales, and LinkedIn.com — one of my favorite things to do is to see who has direct messaged me in LinkedIn since I have started many worthwhile business associations that way — but within thirty minutes, I was focused and concentrating on today's goal.

Do you set short-term as well as long-term goals for yourself? It is helpful to set the long-term goals because, usually, short-term goals will become that much clearer as a stepping stone to accomplishing the long-term goals.

In academia we tend to focus on the short-term goals for our students. In the syllabus we refer to it as "Learning Outcomes." But even for a college course, it is beneficial for faculty, and students, alike to consider the long-term goal for a specific course — how will what a student learns that semester help his or her career goals and even his or her life in general — as well as contributing to one of the goals that I see for college and graduate school, namely, becoming a lifelong learner.

One of the most popular ways to approach goal setting is to apply the acronym S.M.A.R.T., which has been attributed by Duncan Haughey, in his article, "A Brief History of SMART Goals," among others, to consultant George T. Doran and his article introducing the concept in a November 1981 issue of *Management Review*.

Here is what his SMART acronym stands for:

S = Specific

M = Measurable

A = Assignable

R = Realistic

T = Time-related

Let's look at the letters of the acronym further. **Specific** means that you are focusing on one key concern. That is fundamental to my approach to goal-setting as well as how to finish everything that you start. Namely, what is the #1 project, or task, that you want to accomplish rather than a more open-ended "I want to become more productive, get more things done, and finish everything I start that I think still has value."

Instead, you want to be specific: "My goal is to finish the market report that my boss asked me to do on the new product we are considering."

Measurable means that there must be a way of measuring your success at reaching that goal. "My goal is to finish the market report that my boss asked me to do **in three business days.**"

Notice how much more measurable that goal has become.

Assignable refers to who is going to do something. Once again, let us revisit that example included the assignable aspect. "My goal is **for me to finish researching and writing the market report** that my boss asked me to do by the end of business two days from today and **to have it proofread by my assistant by end of business on the third day** on the new product we are considering."

What about **Realistic**, the **R** in the SMART acronym? Is the above-stated goal realistic or is it unrealistic because it should/could really take four to seven days to achieve this goal rather than the projected three days?

In a similar vein, the last letter in the acronym, **T** for **Time-related**, reinforces that having a specific time when the solution could be accomplished is an essential aspect of the SMART approach to goal-setting.

Why not take a few moments to apply the SMART acronym to one of the top projects or tasks, work-related or personal, that you have not yet finished that you really want to complete? Okay here we go.

What is your goal? ________________________________

Now apply SMART to it:

S = Specify (rewrite or revise what you wrote above making sure you are being specific about what you need to finish)

____

M = how will you measure your progress toward achieving this goal?

____

A = who is going to make finishing happen?

R = How long will it take? ______________________

Is that time frame realistic? Yes ____ No ____ If no, what is the true estimate for completion/achieving this goal?

____

T = Now be even more concrete. What is the day or date that you can accomplish this goal?

____

Haughey, in "A Brief History of SMART Goals," notes that some have even expanded SMART to SMARTER. The two additional letters in the revised acronym refer to the following concepts/steps:

E = Evaluated

Considering to what degree the goal has been reached.
A few words about this powerful SMART tool.

R = Reviewed

An additional step in which you reflect on your progress and make any necessary adjustments to your conduct or methodology that may facilitate achieving this goal.

Whether you apply the original SMART or the expanded SMARTER to the #1 task or project that you want to finish — your goal — either acronym are powerful tools for helping you to achieve each of your goals.

What follows is a somewhat detailed self-assessment related to long-term and short-term goals.

A More Detailed Long- and Short-Term Goal Self-Assessment

Use the space below to write down your long-term work and personal goals. Date this information so you can return to these goals down the road as you review if these long-term goals have changed. (In the Appendix there are additional goal-setting sheets for you to use as you revisit your long-term and short-term goals on a regular basis.)

What are some of the long-term work/career goals you might want to list? Going back to school to get an advanced degree? Finishing up a degree or getting a certificate? Becoming CEO of a major or medium-sized company? Starting your own company? Reaching a certain dollar amount in salary? Achieving a specific level in your career?

Long-term Work/Career Goals

Today's date __________

I am currently __________ years of age.

Here are the work/career goals I want to accomplish:

My goal is to ____________________ in 25 years

My goal is to ____________________ in 20 years

My goal is to ____________________ in 15 years

My goal is to ____________________ in 10 years

My goal is to ____________________ in 5 years

My goal is to ____________________ in 2 years

Now let's address your personal goals. Those goals count too and what those goals are, and whether you accomplish those targets, for many, may even influence whether you achieve your work/career goals, or if you must adjust those ambitions. What are some personal goals you might list? Find the love of your life? Start a family? Go on a 2-week family vacation to a dream destination? Plan and attend a high school reunion? Train and run in a marathon? Read 5 classic books that you have always wanted to peruse? Volunteer at a local soup kitchen? Reorganize your closets?

Long-term Personal Goals

Today's date __________

I am currently __________ years of age.

Here are the personal goals I want to accomplish:

My goal is to ____________________ in 25 years

My goal is to ____________________ in 20 years

My goal is to ____________________ in 15 years

My goal is to ____________________ in 10 years

My goal is to ____________________ in 5 years

My goal is to ____________________ in 2 years

Now that you have listed your current work/career long-term goals, let's apply the same exercise to your short-term goals for both work/career and your personal life. One of my favorite time management books of all time, Alan Lakein's 1972 classic, *How to Get Control of Your Time and Your Life* was based on the concept of how I should be spending my time right now! For me, spending this hour, and this day, writing this book is my number one short term work goal (since I finished teaching college on Wednesday and do not return to a classroom for two months, at the end of August.)

Consider your own short-term work/career goals. How should/will you break your time down to increase the likelihood that you will finish everything you start? How about your short-term work/career goals for the next hour? Two hours? Morning? Afternoon? By the end of the work week? By the end of the month? By the end of 3 months? By the end of 6 months? By the end of the year?

As noted before in the SWNS report, Americans are checking their phones 80 times a day. Imagine how much more you could accomplish if you stop checking your phone constantly or at least as frequently as you are checking it? Consider how much more you could get done in the short-term — in the next 30 minutes, hour, 2 hours, morning, afternoon, work day, or even work week?

Use the space below to set your short-term work/career goals up to 1 year. Beyond a year, you are getting into more of a long-term planning consideration.

Short-term Work/Career Goals

Today's date _________

I am currently _________ years of age.

Here are the work/career goals I want to accomplish:

My goal is to ___________________ within 30 minutes

My goal is to ___________________ within 1 hour

My goal is to ___________________ within 2 hours

My goal is to ___________________ by noon

My goal is to ____________________ by 5 PM

My goal is to ____________________ by Friday

My goal is to ____________________ within a month

My goal is to ____________________ within 3 months

My goal is to ____________________ within 6 months

My goal is to ____________________ within 1 year

Now let's apply the same worksheet to your personal short-term goals. Since these are your personal goals, the timing will probably refer to your after-work hours, which will probably be from 6 or 7 PM till you go to sleep, if you work a more traditional 9-5 job, as well as on your weekends and vacation time.

Short-term Personal Goals (After Work)

Today's date __________

I am currently __________ years of age.

Here are the personal goals I want to accomplish:

My goal is to ____________________ within 30 minutes

My goal is to ____________________ within 1 hour

My goal is to ____________________ within 2 hours

My goal is to ____________________ by noon

My goal is to ____________________ by 5 PM

My goal is to ____________________ by bedtime

Short-term Personal Goals (Weekends)

Today's date __________

I am currently __________ years of age.

Here are the personal short-term goals I want to accomplish:

(Related to weekends)

My goal is to ____________________ Friday after work.

My goal is to ____________________ Saturday during the day.

My goal is to ____________________ Saturday in the evening.

My goal is to ____________________ Sunday during the day.

My goal is to ____________________ Sunday in the evening.

Prioritizing

Know the difference between important and must be done versus can be rescheduled or even left undone.

How you prioritize at your job will be determined by so many unique factors. Is it a job that is time-dependent or is it focused more on the achieving the desired product, however long it takes? What priorities you are dealing with in your personal life may also determine how you handle your professional priorities even though we would like to think in an ideal world we have control over everything. For example, a reporter works from home and schedules a phone interview for an article she is writing only to have her three-month old who was supposed be napping to suddenly having a "meltdown." The priority suddenly shifts to dealing with the crying baby.

Use the self-quiz that follows to help yourself with prioritizing if the task or project you are working on is the one to continue with, till you finish it, or if it is in your best interest to switch to doing something else.

SELF-QUIZ

Deciding What to Focus On (and Finish) Now?*

1. On a scale of 1 to 5, how much of a priority is the task I'm evaluating? ___________
2. On a scale of 1 to 5, how much of a priority is the task I'm considering switching to? ___________
3. Rank from 1 to 5 how time sensitive the task I'm doing is compared to the alternative task? ___________
4. Is either task or event a one-time, can't miss opportunity or event, like a wedding or a funeral, or is it repeated on a regular basis? ___________
5. How firm is the deadline for this task on a scale of 1 to 5 with 1 being least firm and 5 most firm? ___________
6. In the short-run, which task has greater benefits, the one I am working on toward finishing or the one I am considering switching to?
7. Who asked you to work on/finish this task? Was it your boss, a co-worker, the boss of your boss or did you make this determination? ___________

*This self-quiz is adapted from *Work Less, Do More: The 7-Day Productivity Makeover.*

There are many ways to approach prioritizing. One of the most popular is the grid or matrix approach that Stephen Covey shares in *The 7 Habits of Highly Effective People.* In Covey's matrix, there are four squares. In the upper left is URGENT and #I. To the right is NOT URGENT and #2. Along the side of the square are the words IMPORTANT and NOT IMPORTANT. In the square below URGENT I is III and to the right, below NOT URGENT II is NOT IMPORTANT IV.

The key is to do the IMPORTANT URGENT and IMPORTANT NOT URGENT activities and to avoid wasting your time in the 3rd and 4th NOT IMPORTANT quadrants. What are in those parts of the matrix? That's where Covey puts the interruptions, busy work, time wasters, and even what he refers to as "some meetings" or "some phone calls."

Another approach to prioritizing is Pareto's 80/20 Rule. This prioritizing tool is a concept that is attributed to the Italian economist Vilfredo Pareto. Back in 1906, he observed that 80 percent the land in his native Italy was owned by only 20 percent of the people. In time, that 80/20 rule got applied to other concepts and eventually to handling time by suggesting that 20 percent of your efforts will give you 80 percent of your results. The key is to figure out what that 20 percent is and to apply it directly to prioritizing, to make sure you're doing the activities that will give you the biggest pay off, whether it is in your business or personal life.

What does prioritizing mean? It means that whatever you are doing is the best use of your time right now. It can be a project, or a relationship, or a task that is of optimum importance to you. That does not always mean it's what you want to do with your time this minute. But it is what you know you should be doing and that is why it is a priority.

Sometimes priorities are imposed on you by your boss or, if you are an entrepreneur and your own boss, by the nature of the job you do. For some, there is little wiggle room in what should be done.

But for others, there are so many choices that it is necessary to continually assess what should be the focus of this morning, this day, this evening, even this minute.

I really like acronyms. Here's one I created for my previous time management book, *Work Less, Do More*. It's my ACTION plan.

A = Assess

C = Control

T = Target

I = Innovate

O = Organize

N! = Now!

Here's how you can apply it to finishing everything you start.

A (Assess) – This is where you look over all the duties that you have that are unfinished and you decide what needs to be done first. As Alan Lakein used to say, what is the best use of your time right now applied to finishing which undertaking?

If you have been asked to speak at a major conference, and last week your speech was a huge success before another audience, you are starting from scratch with this new opportunity. The minute you start making assumptions that performing well in situation A guarantees that you will perform well in situation B, you are setting yourself up for potential failure.

Approach each duty with a freshness, enthusiasm, and commitment to excellence that you applied on Day One, when you started your very first job, or wrote your very first book, and you are more likely to be pleased with each outcome.

That's a longer version of the cliché, "Never assume."

C = **Control**. Focus on what you can influence, namely your own behavior, rather than dwelling on everyone else's or whatever obstacles have been thrown your way. You have competing projects and lots of interruptions and distractions to deal with. But my observation from more than three decades in the time management field is that it is the self-made interruptions that sabotage our optimal use of our time more than the ones imposed by others. You can choose to let your cell phone go to voice mail. You can say "no" to new projects, or other projects, so you can continue to focus on finishing what you have determined is your number 1 priority project.

What are some other ways you can use the C in the ACTION! Strategy to finish the project at hand? If you are overwhelmed with too many assignments, consider relocating, even temporarily, to another location where you focus in on this one project. If your company has a corporate library, perhaps you could go there to think or plan. If your company allows you to telecommute, you might see if you could work an extra day or two in your home office where you might have fewer distractions. By contrast, if you have small children at home and too many distractions, you might consider going to an outside office, if you are a home-based worker, the public library, a coffee shop, or even affiliating with one of the shared workspace alternative office environments that have become so popular, if you can afford it.

T = **Target.** You are going to very much target a specific assignment you are going to finish. Once you finish that one, you can target the next one. The more specific your target, the more likely you are to achieve it. Instead of thinking your target is to write a novel, say you're going to write a sci-fi or historical novel set in India in the 1940s toward the end of British rule.

I = **Innovate.** Be open to trying new things and even fresh ideas or even new technology that might make it faster, easier, or better to finish what you started. Maybe there is a tried-and-true method that you forgot about along the way that you could reapply now?

O = **Organize.** The concept of organizing to improve the speed or even the likelihood that you will finish an assignment ranges from such basic organizing concerns as keeping track of your research to larger issues like grouping similar tasks together, such as doing any necessary phone interviews on the same day or getting into a routine that you work on your priority project every morning, from 9 to noon, so you get a predictable rhythm that increases your productivity.

N! = **Now!** There are a million reasons that you could do something else rather than finish whatever you have targeted as your priority undertaking to complete. The N! in the ACTION! Strategy reminds you that, in most cases, delays reflect procrastinating. What I have observed over the years is that, for most, although they may say that finishing is harder than starting, once they start, most people are amazed that the project that they were procrastinating on moves along faster than they ever dreamed possible. For so many, it is the stalling that is so debilitating. The delay may seem to have justifiable reasons, such as the boss tells you to switch to working on something else, or there is a crisis in customer service that initially you think you are the only one capable of solving. But upon further reflection, often you will discover that one of the 22 beliefs, behaviors, or bad habits discussed in Chapter 2 is at work. Recognize, and deal with, why you are not getting to the priority project Now! and you will be further on the road to selectively completing everything you start.

In the next chapter, Chapter 8, "To-Do Lists That Work," we will explore one of the proven tools to getting things done and finishing up assignments, namely, the to do list. But before you do the exercises in this chapter, or turn to Chapter 8, I want you to return to the Time Log that you have been keeping, beginning in the last chapter.

Look over the Time Log that you put together in the last chapter. That Time Log consists of detailed information about at least one of your work days that you surveyed in the last chapter. Now that you have determined what your priorities are as well as your short and long-term goals, use a highlighter or circle all activities during the day and evening that related to what you need to do, what you must finish.

Are you using some or most of your time toward achieving those ends? Getting those things done? Perhaps you thought you were working on your priority projects but, alas, you were doing a multiplicity of unrelated tasks. Or perhaps you are putting a lot of time and energy into what you need to do, but you are not getting things finished as quickly as you would like. Read on! The information you are gathering about yourself should be useful as you gain greater self-mastery over your time and, along with that improvement, the ability to finish everything you start.

Prioritizing the Unfinished

Not all unfinished projects or concerns are equal in importance. It is up to you to sort that out. Sometimes other people do it for you, like when your boss comes into your office, or enters your cubicle and says, "Put aside whatever it is you're doing. I need this done in an hour."

To sort out the various tasks, projects, or concerns that you have that are unfinished, and how to reorganize what you will do next, make a list for yourself. You can have one list for business unfinished concerns and another list for personal ones.

Next to each item, put "Reason for delay" as well as the "Consequence if You Fail to Finish."

Think about each and every item on your lists and decide if you should continue or quit and, if you decide it needs to be finished, in what order?

You can also give it a time frame: immediately, by end of business today, by the end of the week, by the end of the month, within 6 months, within the year, within 5 years, and so on.

Here's a sample list that you might find useful as a prototype for your list.

> Business project, task, or concern to do
>
> ______________________________
>
> Is this something you want to do or it is an assignment?
>
> ______________________________
>
> What are the potential consequences if you fail to finish it?
>
> ______________________________
>
> On a scale of 1 to 10 with 1 least important and 10 most vital, how important is it to you to finish it?
>
> ______________________________
>
> If you decide you must finish it, what is the time frame?
>
> ______________________________

Do this for everything on your list of business or personal tasks or issues that you want to finish.

Once you have gone through each and every task, assign a number value to each one, prioritizing everything by significance, beginning with #1 until you hit the top number on your list.

Reorder your list to match the numbers tackling #1 first.

Date the lists and revisit the lists as you finish each item. As circumstances change, however, be flexible enough to remove certain items from your lists and to add others.

EXERCISES

1. Use the ACTION! Strategy worksheet in the Appendix to apply it to your priority project or task that you want to finish.
2. Take the time to simplify your goal-setting ideas and write down your #1 goals in three areas: a work or school goal; a personal goal; a goal about finishing a project.

   Work (or school) goal: ______________________

   Personal goal: ______________________

   Finishing goal: ______________________

   Now go back and apply the SMART acronym to each one:

   Work goal ______________________

   S = specific ______________________

   M – measurable ______________________

   A = achievable ______________________

R = realistic ______________________________

T = time-bound ____________________________

Personal goal ______________________________

S = specific ________________________________

M – measurable ____________________________

A = achievable _____________________________

R = realistic ______________________________

T = time-bound ____________________________

Finishing goal _____________________________

S = specific ________________________________

M – measurable ____________________________

A = achievable _____________________________

R = realistic ______________________________

T = time-bound ____________________________

CHAPTER 8

To-Do Lists That Work

I remember interviewing a woman who discovered the solution to her insomnia was writing down what she had to do the next day before she went to bed each night. Having that concrete list helped her sleep. Without that list, she had free-floating anxiety throughout the night as she ruminated about, "What should I do tomorrow? What do I have to do? What am I forgetting that I must accomplish?"

Maybe you do not need a to-do list, so you can sleep better at night, but for most of us, whether you create and keep a to-do list regularly, or frequently, or only do it when you are in a real organizational or time crunch and need that extra clarity and structure, the to-do list is a useful tool to finishing everything you start.

Earlier I shared a to-do list that did not work. It was basically a list of the 47 things I had to accomplish, from major projects to everyday chores. A to-do list that long fails as an organizing and self-management tool. Although all that information might be useful to have in one place, it is necessary to create a to-do list that is realistic and manageable.

One of the key aspects of a to-do list is the element of time. It is key not just to list a specific project or task that you must do, but when will you do it and how long it will take. Also, how will you indicate that you have finished it? Cross it off your list? Have a separate box that you check off?

Here is the one biggest trap that too many to-do list makers fall into: if you do not complete everything on your current to-do list, it is essential to move that incomplete item to the next to-do list. Avoid letting that item languish on the old list, undone, and, before you know it, falling between the cracks and getting into the "limbo" category of unfinished items or even larger projects.

A sample of a to-do list follows. A few additional blank to-do lists are in the Appendix for you to photocopy and use. You may also purchase to-do lists at the office supply store, in person or over the Internet.

MY TO-DO LIST

Today's date ____________________

To do	Time to complete	Completed (date)
Projects (or tasks within one project)		
#1 ____________	____________	____________
#2 ____________	____________	____________
#3 ____________	____________	____________
#4 ____________	____________	____________
#5 ____________	____________	____________
#6 ____________	____________	____________
Chores (or errands)		
#1 ____________	____________	____________
#2 ____________	____________	____________
#3 ____________	____________	____________

If you have Microsoft Excel on your computer, you could also create a To-Do list using that software. On the left in column A is what you need to do. In column you could put a description of the task. In column C you could insert how long you think it will take. In column D, you could put a check mark and in column E, you could insert the date that you complete the task.

What's important is to have a written record and guide for what you need to do. This is like my suggestion to college students that they take notes during class which, for too many, has become a lost art and skill. Research has discovered that taking notes by hand has a better outcome than notetaking on a computer or an electronic device. It is my opinion that taking notes on a computer is better than not taking notes at all. But, if possible, taking notes by hand has a lot of positive benefits. This ties in with the advantages of writing, and keeping, a to-do list. There is something about writing things down that makes it real and strengthens your commitment to accomplishing something. That does not mean that writing it down substitutes for doing it. You must do what you put on your "to do" list.

But writing down what you are committing to finish on your to do list will help you concretize those goals and to get each one done. A well-constructed to-do list will also help you monitor your progress.

We noted in the last couple of chapters that goal setting benefits from realistic deadlines. The more information you have about how long something really takes to complete, the better your chance of setting a realistic deadline in the first place. Recording that information on your to-do list – how long it does take to complete – will provide you with a record of your productivity.

If you are self-employed or a consultant who is paid by the hour, the more information you have about just how much you accomplish in an hour, the more realistic you can be about your pricing for a project.

Let's discuss how you might organize your list. There are two main ways:

- Chronologically
- By importance

If you organize your list chronically, you will take yourself through your day and evening, noting what you will do from morning till sleep time.

If you prefer to organize by importance, your list will be ordered by the ranking that you give to tasks, regardless of time.

"But I am not a list maker!" you might be thinking or saying out loud. Do you ever make a grocery list to take shopping? If not, you may be spending more time and money at the store. Shopping lists help with planning and accomplishing more in less time at the supermarket.

In a similar way, using a list for organizing your major project or projects will help you to get more done.

If you have a huge project that you need to finish, you might need to have interim tasks, as well as multiple deadlines, within the overall task. For example, planning the annual retreat is just too big a category to have as the "one" item to check off on your to-do list. The overall project might be "plan the annual retreat" but for a specific day, you might have these tasks on your to-do list:

1. E-mail and/or talk with last year's planner and find out contact information for the venue they used if we are going to return there.
2. Explore alternative venues through google or contacting the company travel planner.
3. Check in with ________________ in human resources about the head count for the event.
4. Find out what day and date has been firmed up and whether there is any flexibility on that date.
5. Pick a date for the brainstorming session for the annual retreat committee to meet and discuss the theme for this year's retreat.
6. Once the date for the brainstorming session is selected, pick a date for the meeting.

7. Write an e-mail invitation to the brainstorming session.
8. Share the invitation with another committee member for feedback.
9. Once approved, send out the e-mail invitation.
10. Go to the website for last year's retreat's printers for information sheets and imprinted giveaways.
11. Request sample giveaways.

Your goal is not to become someone who makes up lists. Instead, you are creating, and monitoring, your to-do list as a way of maximizing your efficiency and increasing the likelihood that you get a project finished and OTD (Out the Door), another one of my acronyms and one of my favorites.

EXERCISES

1. Write a very simple to do list for today whether it is a workday or a weekend/leisure day. What organizing principle will you use? Chronologically? By importance?

To Do List for Today

Today's date ____________________ Day of the week ________

1. ____
2. ____
3. ____
4. ____
5. ____

Tomorrow, review this list. How many items on it did you accomplish? Did your organizing principle help you to accomplish all that you had to do?

2. If you find writing down what you must do on paper does not work for you, what other system, if any, will you use? Take the time to explore some of the electronic to-do list options that are listed in this book's Resources in the back. I personally prefer to write a to do list on my computer, smartphone, or on paper, but there are many who swear by the electronic options—some are free, and some require a monthly or annual fee — to help keep their daily or weekly "to do" goals organized.

CHAPTER 9

Learning to Say "No"

Few people like to be rejected and to most, hearing a "no" could be perceived as a rejection. Especially if you have a need to please everyone or, even more importantly, if you have trouble hearing the word "no," you may also have trouble saying "no."

Having that challenge may land you in the position of saying "yes" too often so that, before you know it, you find yourself having too much to do. That situation causes you not to finish the projects you need to complete.

One cure may be learning to say "no" more often. You must use your judgment on this. You might be totally comfortable saying "no" to a co-worker who asks you to help with his or her work, even though it is not your job, but if the boss asks you to drop everything and switch gears as you work on another project, saying "no" may not be the wise option.

The reason I am focusing in on this challenge in a separate chapter is that it is as pivotal to say "no" in a way that does not offend as it is to turn something or someone down. If you say "no" in such a way that you create hostility, or you are seen as someone who is shrugged off additional work, saying "no" in the short run may backfire in the long run.

So, you want to say "no" in a way that is polite and that acknowledges and respects the needs and priorities of the person who is asking you to devote your time and focus to a request. Learning to say "no" relates to goal-setting and prioritizing. Is the request that you are being asked to do in line with your professional or personal goals? Will saying "yes" help you to accomplish your own priorities? Will saying "yes" get you closer to your goal of finishing whatever it is that you started?

If the answer is "no," then if possible, say "no" but say it in a way the communicates you are not rejecting the person or their request, but that you are simply committed to finishing something else at this time. You may even say something like, I'd be happy to help as soon as I'm finished with this particular project.

Another way to say "no" with a reduced likelihood of alienating the person who is asking for your help is to offer someone else as an alternative. Most people, when they ask you to do something, are just looking for someone – anyone – to solve their problem. If you will not incur the wrath of the person to whom you send this person for an alternative possible "yes," making a suggestion for one or more ways that they can get assistance will help reduce the disappointment at your "no."

You might be able to suggest an organization, association, or a company, rather than an individual, so you are less likely to get a specific person annoyed at you for volunteering him or her unless you have check it out with that individual in advance.

You could also suggest another department at your own company if they might be a better option or if you know that they might even welcome a specific opportunity.

If you have a tendency to say "yes" when you really wanted to say "no" you may have a deep-seated childhood need to please. This could stem from when you were a child and wanted to make your mother or father feel as if you are cooperative and deserving of their love and attention. Now, as an adult, you can't seem to stop yourself from duplicating that type of a reaction in the workplace or business situations. At least give yourself some time to think about any request that will take up your time and shift your focus. "Let me consider your request and get back to you," is a response that will buy you time.

After you have gotten that reprieve, you can run the request by a trusted friend, family member, or even co-worker, if you feel that is a safe option. If they know how busy you are, and that you have one or more priority projects that you really need to focus on finishing, they might help you to see that saying "no" is your best course of action. With their reinforcement about what you should do or, if you just use the time to think it through yourself, with your own reflection on what you should do, you can rehearse how you will say "no." If you take a day or two to consider the request, and you decide to say "no," it might be less offensive than if you have a knee jerk "no" which might seem as if you are indifferent to whoever is asking for your help.

There are times when you might want to say "yes." It could be a great opportunity but if you have a finishing challenge, you might have to put some time parameters on your "yes."

For example, as we mentioned before, you could say, "Thanks so much for the opportunity you are offering me. I would love to help, but I have several projects I must first finish first. If you could wait until they are completed, I can then get to your request. Would that work for you?" The key is that you are not completely turning someone or something down but pushing it off into the future (so you can attend currently to your own priority projects that you want to finish now).

Here are 20 ways to graciously say "no" including the ones noted above:

20 WAYS TO SAY NO GRACIOUSLY*

*These statements are reprinted, with permission, some in slightly edited form, with five additional ways added, from my book, *Work Less, Do More*.

1. "No but thank you very much for the offer."
2. "I don't think so, but can I get back to you in a couple of weeks when I have caught up on my work?"
3. "I really want to say "yes," but I unfortunately just have to say "no." I hope you understand."
4. "Let me consider your offer and get back to you." (When

you get back to the person the next day or two, then you politely say "no.")

5. "I am very grateful for the vote of confidence you are showing in me by asking for my help. Unfortunately, for a variety of time and other reasons, I have to politely decline."
6. "Unfortunately, I have a conflicting commitment for that date. I deeply regret that I therefore have to decline."
7. "I'm sorry, but please understand that I have to be firm about this since I have said "no" to you before. Unfortunately, I still have to say "no." Thanks for respecting my decision."
8. "I think so highly of you and your association [company, organization, event, etc.], but I'm unable to accept your gracious offer."
9. I'm so sorry I have to decline but I'm on deadline."
10. "I'm flattered that you asked me but, unfortunately, I have to decline."
11. "I'm unavailable now. Would you get back to me on ________________ [fill in the time or even a specific date] when we could revisit the situation in case I might be able to say "yes" at that time?"
12. "I just accepted another assignment that won't allow me to devote the time to your project that I would need to do a quality job."
13. "Unfortunately, I can't accept, but would you like me to suggest someone else for you to contact and consider?"
14. "Thank you but unfortunately I have to say "no."
15. "I wish I could be in two places at once but, alas, I have

already accepted another invitation for the very same time and date but in another location."

16. "Sorry, I am going away on a trip and I am trying to finish up everything on my plate before I leave. Do you want to contact me again after I return?"

17. "I don't think so but let me consider your offer more carefully and get back to you in a few weeks if you are able to wait that long for my decision."

18. "No, not now. It's not a good time for me. Maybe later."

19. "Maybe another time. You caught me at a bad time."

20. "No, because _______________ [insert reason here]."

In the next chapter, we will explore how you could possibly delegate some or all that you need to finish to free yourself up for what only you can do.

EXERCISES

1. Think back to the last day, week, month or even longer. What is the last thing you said "yes" to that, in hindsight, you really should have said "no" to instead? Write that situation down here.

   ____

   What were the negative or positive consequences to you professionally and personally for that "yes?"

   ____

   Based on what you learned in this chapter, replay what happened when you were initially asked to do whatever it is that you regret saying "yes" to. Right down the "no" answer that you could have given and that you are hopefully more likely to say next time it is in your best interest to say "no" not "yes."

2. As noted earlier in the chapter, those who have a hard time saying "no" often have a difficult time "hearing" "no." When is the last time you heard "no' and it upset you?

____

How long ago did this happen?

____

Do you think the way the "no" that you received made you feel could be behind why you say "yes" too often?

____

CHAPTER 10

Becoming a Better Delegator

Besides an inability to say "no," those who have too many unfinished projects or activities often are trying to do everything themselves. Time managers agree that the most efficient use of your time is to do what you do best and what no one else can do, as well as you or in the same way. That means that there are many instances when you should and could be delegating some tasks so you are freed up to focus on what you truly need to finish.

Here are some of the tell-tale signs that you should be delegating more, in general or related to a specific task:

1. A task is beneath your skills level.
2. You are bored by some or all aspects of a task that you do.
3. A computer or another form of technology could do what you have been doing.
4. You planned to delegate a task, but you decided it would be faster to do it yourself than to train someone.
5. You distrust that anyone can handle some or many aspects of your job as well as you.
6. You have been told more than once that you are a "control freak" who prefers to do everything himself/herself.

Do one or more of the above statements describe you? If you see yourself in any of those statements, you will have to do some real self-talk or consider working with someone who specializes in these matters to become more comfortable delegating to others.

I am not going to paint an unrealistic picture of delegating. It is not without its challenges. The time that you save by having some or many of the tasks you usually do, that could free up your time to get more projects finished, can also open a pandora's box of concerns. I am reminded of the famous historian who delegated research to one or more of her research assistants. Unfortunately, they did not put quotation marks around many of the paragraphs that they quoted directly from books or documents. When the historian wrote her book, assuming those quotes were paraphrased, original words, not plagiarized ones, several paragraphs that were indeed quoted verbatim without giving credit were picked up by plagiarism software. The historian figured out what happened and apologized for what her research assistants had done. But it still damaged her reputation, even if temporarily, which until that point had been unblemished.

When it works, however, delegating is a real time saver, allowing you to free up valuable time and resources to finish that priority project that you never seem to get around to. Or, if you do get to it, you are devoting far fewer hours to it than you know could help move it along faster.

As associate broker at Image Realty, Beverly DePew, checked off in my survey as the number one reason she might leave a task or project unfinished, "I should be delegating a particular task or project to someone else." She expanded on that concept, adding, "Too often there are tasks that my administrative assistant or even the buyer in a transaction could do, but I do instead. Maybe that's a control issue to make sure all tasks get done, but I know in my mind someone else could have completed the task. However, the overwhelming pile of "to-do's" gets my time management off balance."

DePew is not alone. Delegating that task or project to someone else in the first place, and getting it off your plate, could be the way to free up time to finish the priority ventures that only you can do. Here are some steps to take if you want to delegate more effectively:

8 STEPS TO MORE EFFECTIVE DELEGATING

1. Decide what tasks, aspects of a project, or entire projects that you are willing to delegate.

Delegate what you dislike doing or that someone else could do as well, or perhaps even better, then you.

2. Select the best person to whom you will be delegating.

Screen this potential person carefully. You will require a resume but interview him or her by phone and, if possible, in person as well. If this is going to be a remote position, use Skype or FaceTime to interview the potential candidate so you have more than just words to judge him or her by. See if there are any red flags in the resume that need to be checked out. If possible, ask the potential person you will be delegating to complete a sample task that is like what he/she will be doing on a regular basis. Review that sample, carefully, before you commit to hiring that person or even allowing someone in another part of the company to transfer over to you.

3. Develop trust in the person to whom you are delegating.

Especially in the beginning, check over his/her work and make sure it conforms to the sample that you approved. If possible, have another employee review the work by the person you are delegating to, so you have a second opinion. If any changes must be made, see how he/she handles feedback and how quickly, and accurately, those corrections are carried out.

4. Make sure your instructions are clear.

You are ultimately responsible for the work of the person you delegate to, so you need to be an excellent teacher. Be overly cautious about delegating if you realistically lack the teaching skills that you need. If necessary, ask a co-worker or someone else who reports to you to help you with the training, so the outcome will be an excellent one.

5. Make what you delegate very clear and have a firm completion date as well as a follow-up date for discussion.

Too often, once the initial commitment is made to someone to whom a major task or multiple duties are being delegated, the follow-up is rare or too open ended. Have a specific date for following up as well as completing the assignment. The more specific you are, the better. The follow-up will be in two days. The completion date for this part of the project will be by this date. Arrange to discuss the work highlighting what is positive and what needs to be improved.

6. Give credit and praise, when earned.

You could praise the person you delegate to privately or, if appropriate, you could share with your team the role that person is playing in a project. For example, at the weekly team meeting, if you have started delegating verifying contact information for the recipients of a report that you are finalizing, you could say, "I want to thank So-and-So for doing such an excellent job verifying all the names, e-mail addresses, and current phone numbers for those who will receive our report, once it is finalized. That work assures that we can get the report out faster, and with more confidence that the recipient contact information is up-to-date, because of those efforts." Or you could give credit, privately and confidentially. "Thanks for your help. You are doing a noteworthy job."

7. Delegate responsibility for the job, not just one task.

Be careful that you are not making more work for yourself by delegating. The idea is that if you delegate more effectively, you truly will save time and be able to devote more of your quality hours to finishing up the tasks that only you can do. Keep checking up on the person you delegate to until you feel confident that you can give him/her full responsibility for that task and the entire job that it is part of. Referring to the delegating of the contact information for the report recipients, the person to whom that task was delegated should also be entering the data into an Excel spreadsheet or the company database. If you must take that data and enter it yourself, you are being pulled into that job which should have included that task as well as the research aspect of it. In that way, the task of researching and updating the database will be done, from start to finish, by the person to whom you delegated.

8. Consider delegating to technology, not just people.

You usually must train, and manage, the people to whom you delegate. There is another option in addition to delegating to individuals, or lieu of that approach, namely using various types of technology to get some entire tasks done or parts of tasks that you used to do manually or all by yourself. In the Resource section in this book I list a range of apps and websites that you may delegate everything from keeping track of your to-do lists to helping you to set goals. Buying a dedicated robot might be outside of your budget right now, but there are versions of robots that you could rent or purchase such as the robotic vacuums like iRobot Roomba that can help relieve you of some of your cleanup chores. Once considered somewhat tawdry, sending invitations electronically, including RSVPs recorded automatically, have become much more fashionable and in vogue for business and personal events. Using these services can free up untold hours addressing envelopes and manually keeping track of attendees.

In the next chapter we will see how the FINISH acronym as well as everything you have been learning in this book is applied to a sample major task: finishing the writing of a book.

EXERCISES

1. Make a list of tasks that you are doing yourself and, in the right column, to whom you might delegate it.

Task	To Whom Might I Delegate It?
__________	________________________________
__________	________________________________
__________	________________________________
__________	________________________________

2. There are some predictable situations that occur when you delegate. If you plan for how you will handle these developments, you might feel more confident about trying, or even expanding, who and what you are delegating.
   - The person you are delegating to has had one too many spelling errors or typos in their work lately. What should you do about it?
   - Taking too long is the criticism you have of the person you are delegating to. How might you suggest he/she speed up their productivity without compromising on accuracy?
   - The person you are delegating to gets too many personal phones calls on his/her smartphone as well as far too many text messages that you know are unrelated to work. Should you say something? If you should, what would you say?
   - Although you are pleased with the work that the person you are delegating to is doing, you think you should have a more regular schedule for conferring and discussing her/his progress. When do you suggest such a meeting? Where would it take place? What will be the frequency? How can you present this regular review in a positive light without the person you delegate to feeling as if you are criticizing his/her work or looking over his/her shoulder?

CHAPTER 11

An Example of Finally Finishing a Major Effort: Writing a Book

When I was an editor at Grove Press, Inc., I read a novel by a young man that I thought was outstanding. I asked Barney Rosset, the founder and president of the company, if I could acquire it, he agreed, we decided on the advance to offer, and I made an offer to that young man. It had been his lifelong dream to get a novel published.

But he preferred to do a rewrite of that novel before going forward with the deal. I patiently waited for him to complete his rewrite. Unfortunately, after a period, we both realized that he was just not going to let himself finish that book, so the deal was never finalized.

That is just one example of a writing career that ended before it began. There are numerous other unpublished authors who need help in finishing their first book. There are also a number of authors who have published one or more books, but they are procrastinating on finishing the next one. They need help finishing as well. If you fall into either of these categories of authors, this chapter is for you.

Failing to finish, and publish, that first, or subsequent, books takes its toll on a frustrated author. But it can also make it tough on an author's family members and friends, who feel helpless as their loved ones ruminate about their unfinished manuscripts. If the book is under contract, there are editors, and production departments, that are being kept waiting. If it is book that is being written on speculation, or that will be self-published, failing to achieve the goal of having a completed manuscript that you can publish still has emotional, financial, and professional consequences.

If you are an unpublished author with an unfinished book manuscript, or you are a published author with one or more incomplete manuscripts that need to get finished, here are 21 ways to help you get that manuscript completed and OTD (Out the Door).

21 Ways to Help Yourself to Finish Writing Your Book*

1 Remember the time management principle of breaking up a big task into little tasks, little steps.

This principle applies to writing, and finishing, a book. Writing a book sounds like a daunting task, and it is. It means writing anywhere from 40,000 to 70,000 words. It can mean researching and writing ten chapters, for nonfiction, or 25 chapters, for fiction. So, divide up your book into more manageable parts.

Here are some ways:

Decide on how many words you will write in a day. Perhaps it will be 5,000 or 1,000 or, if you already know what you want to say, as many as 10,000. In 5 days, you could have your first draft!

If the word count method does not work for you, try breaking up your table of contents into chapters and working on a chapter at a time, for nonfiction.

For fiction, figure out how you will approach your novel. Will you write the whole thing out or do an outline? Will you work on a chapter at a time or try to write a certain number of words per day?

The most important point is that by breaking down your book into more manageable smaller pieces you are more likely to get it finished!

---

*This is an expanded, edited, and updated version of the two-part article I wrote entitled, "How to Overcome Your Procrastination and Finish Writing Your Book," that was published in www.Indiereader.com on February 1 and February 8, 2016.

2 Decide if You Are Procrastinating About Finishing Your Book or You Are Justified in Taking More Time.

As the author of six books on time management, including *Put More Time on Your Side* and *Work Less, Do More*, I have researched and coached about procrastination for decades. What I tell my workshop attendees, and readers, is that it's key to decide if your delay – procrastination—is because you're avoiding finishing, or you need the time to get more information or to productively improve your project. Apply those concepts to finishing up your book: Are you afraid of finishing because if you don't finish, you can't be judged and possibly criticized? Or do you need more time to do more research, improve your writing with another rewrite or two, or maybe you have another project that is timelier that must be finished first?

Once you understand what is causing your procrastination – or your delay in finishing your book – it will be easier to apply some of the proven techniques for overcoming procrastination to finishing your book.

3 Plan a reward for finishing the book.

If you have a publisher, you will hopefully be rewarded with an acceptance and even the second part of your advance, but whether or not you have a publisher for your new book, reward yourself for completing it. Pick something that means something to you and make a commitment to making that happen once you finish your book. Buy tickets to a Broadway show you've been putting off because you didn't want to make plans until your book was finished. Or promise yourself that you'll go on that weekend trip that you've been putting off. Perhaps you'll take a cooking course or donate your time at a homeless shelter because you won't have "the book" taking up all your time and energy.

4 Write down a list of pluses for finishing your book.

Make a list of as many of the positive results of completing your book that you can think of and put it in a prominent place in your office. For example, a renowned sociologist wrote to me, when I told him that I had finally finished my dissertation. I'm paraphrasing what he wrote, but this is the core of it is that now I would no longer have to explain to anyone why I was still working on my dissertation. The same is true for books. I remember when my very first nonfiction book was published. It was called *The Vegetable Passion: The History of the Vegetarian State of Mind*. Scribner's published it when I was 26 years old. I had started the research for that book as a junior in college, researching a speech on the history of vegetarianism. My research had continued over many years, including trips to India and Germany, and teaching a course on the subject at The New School. When I told my mother that I had finally finished writing the book, she blurted out something like, "I thought that book was published already."

Some pluses for finishing a nonfiction book? A way to spread your brand. A demonstration of your expertise that can lead to TV, radio, and press interviews. If you write fiction, finishing your novel or short story collection can lead to a movie deal. It's a way to share your plot and characters with others besides yourself. Let's also not forget that there is the possibility of making money from book sales.

5 By finishing, you avoid the possibility that you will become bored with the project and put it aside forever.

To finish a book, you need a momentum. Here's the challenge: to start, continue and finish a book-length project, you also need to pace yourself. Although I wrote the first draft of two of my novels in a week and a weekend, respectively, the editing and rewriting took weeks and even years to finish each book. But the key is to keep with a project, for as long as it takes, to complete the book. That could be days, months, or years. Avoid putting your book aside for too long or it may languish forever or, especially in the case of non-fiction works that are timely, it could become stale and out-of-date before it's even published.

6 Is your perfectionism stopping you from finishing?

I was having a hard time finishing my book *Victims*, the result of four years of original research into crime victims including completing a two-year program and getting a master's in criminal justice from Goddard College. I was rereading the galleys of the book that was already accepted by my publisher, Scribner's. But I wanted to make some changes. Nothing drastic but I wanted to do some rewriting. As anyone who has worked with a major house before knows, publisher do not like changes at this point in the project. Not only is it costly, in many cases, to make changes but every time you make a change, you open the possibility that you will create another error since the book has been proofread and "signed off on" by the editor, proofreader, and, presumably at this point, the author.

So, I contacted my first boss in publishing, Nancy Creshkoff, who had also become a friend and I asked her advice. She'd been in publishing for decades including as a project editor in the school division at Macmillan Publishing Company. Nancy told me that I could rewrite that one book forever, or I could accept the fact that this book was finished, I had learned a lot by writing, and finishing it, as writers learn something from each of the books that we write. But I would stop rewriting this one and apply what I learned to the next book I wrote.

I took Nancy's advice and gave the go ahead to my publisher to print and publish *Victims* which got rave reviews and had an impact on victims, criminologists, sociologists, and victim advocates because the book was published at the right time.

7 Imagine the worst thing that could happen if you finish your book and see yourself surviving it.

What do you dread the most about finishing your book? Getting a negative review? Putting in all that work and even getting great reviews but meager sales?

For every book author, there will be a different fear, or two. The key is for you to take the time, if you're having a problem with finishing a book, to sit down and doing some self-talk about your worst fears that may be stopping you from finishing.

Then see yourself overcoming those fears. A bad review? Okay, it happens, from time to time. But you will get over it. If most of the reviews are positive, hopefully the negative one won't carry as much weight as you're giving it in your mind to the point of letting it stop you from finishing and publishing your book.

Great reviews, on Amazon, Barnes and Noble, Goodreads, and elsewhere, but meager sales? Okay, that also happens. But if you finish your book, and get it published, you at least have the chance of someday having great sales. You can't sell a manuscript that's sitting in your drawer or languishing on your hard drive. You need to finish your book and get it out there.

8 Aim for excellence, not a perfection that is unrealistic.

There is a caveat to this statement/solution. When I give speeches on time management, and I discuss when perfectionism is a time waster, it usually gets a laugh when I say that you want a brain surgeon and a proofreader to be perfectionists. So, there is a place for perfectionism in writing and finishing a book. Whether you are self-publishing or being published by a commercial house, you want your finished book to be edited and proofread to perfection. But as the book author, you must aim for excellence in your role, rather than an unrealistic perfectionism that may be behind doing the 15th rewrite on your manuscript when you were finished when you did your seventh rewrite.

9 Please yourself first.

A useful rule of thumb in writing books is to first please yourself. If you've pleased yourself – and, if you set and achieve very high standards for yourself – then you will be more secure about the book you are finishing and less traumatized by a fear of what your editor, the public, or critics will think of it.

Still not ready to finish up that manuscript and get it OTD – Out the Door? Read on!

10 Treat every book as a separate project without comparing it to previous books or worrying about future ones.

They used to say in the book publishing world that it's harder to get a second book published than a first one. That's because when you publish your first book, you're a first-time author. No expectations. Nothing to compare that book to. But once you've published one book, now you've got your experiences related to your first book – or your previous works – to motivate you or discourage you when it comes to finishing up this current manuscript.

Stop doing that! Forget about those comparisons! Every book that you write does and should stand on its own, even if it's part of a series. Don't let the comparisons that others might make about you and your various books slow you down or even stop you in your tracks from finishing this new book. Treat every book like a self-contained project. (It's like the parent of more than one child. When asked who's their favorite child, they will hopefully answer, "Both," or "Each one.")

11 No one cares as much as you do about when or even if you finish this book.

Even your publisher, if you have one, may not care about you finishing this manuscript as much as you do. Your publisher will care about the money that they advance to and publishing your book, but it's your career that's at stake. It's your reputation as an author.

To you, this manuscript that you're unable to finish could be the next big step in your career. It could help you to get a promotion at work or, if you are an academic, to get tenure at the university where you teach.

This new book could fulfill a lifelong commitment to yourself to "write a book," or it could be a way to share your unique story with your family and friends, if it's a memoir.

By finishing this manuscript, it will be a way to free up all the time and energy you've been putting into this book project whether you now use that time to start a new book, go on a trip, spend more time with family and friends, or just read more for pleasure now that your book is done.

Generating the internal pressure to keep going and finish your book is the best drive toward finishing that you can have. Finishing up a book is somewhat like running a race.

Don't give up your dream of finishing this book. You *can* do it!

12 Give up the myth that "I don't have time to write."

You do have the time to write even if you have a fulltime job or you are a fulltime caregiver. Once you make the commitment to writing, no matter how busy you are, you will be amazed at how much time you have available to you. Here are just some suggestions that will enable you to make the time to write, even if you cannot write during the work day:

Wake up an hour earlier (without making yourself sleep

deprived.)

Go to sleep an hour or two later.

Turn off the TV at night and put in an hour or two for writing instead.

On the weekends, devote at least one to three hours a day to writing.

If you are a fulltime caregiver, consider hiring a part-time babysitter or elder care companion to free up one or more hours a day so you can write.

If you commute to work, write on the train or bus.

If you drive to work, consider talking into your smartphone and electronically turning those words into manuscript pages or transcribing your recorded words by yourself or farming it out to a transcription service.

Hire an editor, ghostwriter, or writing coach to help you finish up your book.

Repeat this phrase again, "I can make the time to write."

13 Allow for delays.

I am suggesting that sometimes you must put that book aside and return to it hours, days, months, and, in rare instances, even years down the road. The big challenge is knowing when those delays are in the service of your book and not just procrastination because of your reluctance to finish. Here's the tricky part. You can't force passion and, even with creative nonfiction, passion will help your writing to sing and soar and not be mundane and boring. So, if you must take a few hours off to walk the dog, recharge your batteries by getting together with friends, or reconnect with your romantic partner, it just might help your writing. *But get back to the manuscript and finish!*

14 *Don't* allow for delays.

On the other hand, sometimes you must make the very difficult decision that you have to avoid a delay because it just might

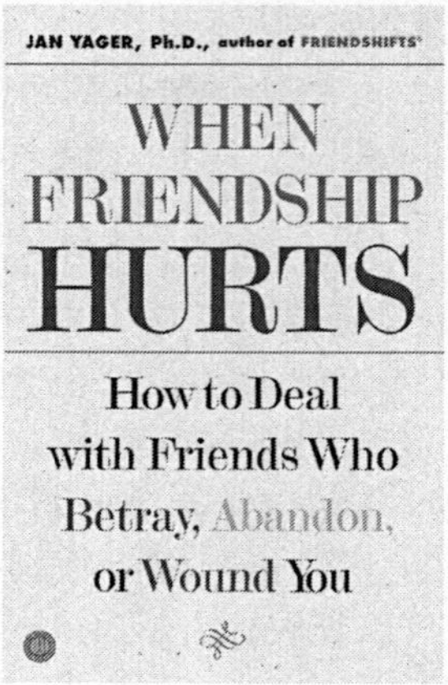

sink your project when you're close to finishing.

That's what happened to me when I was literally in the home stretch with my book, *When Friendship Hurts*, which was under contract with Simon & Schuster. I had bought airline tickets, and reserved a hotel room, to attend the BookExpo which was in Chicago at that time. I was really looking forward to the trip. It was going to be my reward for finishing my book. But, alas, I wasn't finished yet. But I was on a writing roll and, those of you who have written a book, or are writing a book, know what that means. It's what I call being "in the zone" and it's a wonderful time when you truly are about to finish a book that has taken one or more years to write.

So, I made the very difficult decision to cancel my trip, including losing out on the nonrefundable airfare from New York. But I know that I had to put finishing that book first and because of that, I finished that weekend, delivered the book the following week, and the rest, as they say, is history. That book went on to excellent reviews, TV interviews on *Good Morning America*, and other major shows, going into seven printings – it's still selling after more than a decade and the e-book has a new introduction – and getting translated into 29 languages.

So, you must be the judge of whether you will allow for delays. If your friends and family understand how huge the challenge is of finishing a book, they will understand if you can't see them temporarily because of the point you're at in writing (and finishing up) your book.

15 If you don't have a deadline imposed by someone else, create one for yourself.

Deadlines are useful rather than something to be dreaded. It helps you to focus and have a goal. You need to create a deadline that is realistic and possible. Too far in the future and it can lead to procrastination. Too soon and it can stress you out or even lead you to finish before you take the necessary time that you need to do the job that your book requires. With a long writing project like a book, especially if this is your first book, figuring out a deadline for finishing that is realistic may take some trial and error.

You might also need to have interim deadlines. Instead of one master deadline – and this will especially work if you are going to be published by a traditional publisher and they've given you one main deadline, such as delivering the entire book by a certain date—create deadlines for each chapter. This fits in with one of the key time management principles: divide complex tasks into smaller units. So, a book with twenty chapters, will have at least twenty deadlines, one distinct target time frame per chapter.

16 Consider if fear of failure is behind your incomplete manuscript.

Reread Chapter 2, "The Reasons for Failing to Finish Are Within You," especially the section on "Fear of Failure," as the reason you are failing to complete your manuscript. Having a fear of failure is common in most people but for authors, especially since the rise of amazon and reader reviews makes it possible to have a negative review denouncing your work for all to see, this fear must be faced, and overcome.

There is a classic book by Susan Jeffers, Ph.D. with one of those great titles that says it all: *Feel the Fear and Do It Anyway.* That is precisely what you need to do as a book author if you are to get this manuscript finished and published. It might not be the great book you had hoped it could be. It might not be "The Great American Novel," as that first novel is often referred to by aspiring novelists. But your nonfiction book just might be a blockbuster that contributes a concept and phrase to everyday speech, like Malcolm Gladwell's *The Tipping Point*, or a self-published novel, like Andrew Weir's *The Martian*, that goes on to sell millions of copies and to become a hit movie.

You do not know what will happen with this manuscript that you are writing. You cannot predict if it will be well-received, a blockbuster, or a bust, but you need to finish it, and publish it, to find out. Have courage. Get out from behind your words and share those words with the world. You will feel better when you do that. Make sure your book is the best book it could possibly be but at the point you feel you have done your best, at the point in the writing process where you know you are finished, you need to take the next step, and, despite any fear of failure, you need to let it go and to let it get published.

17 Don't let a Fear of Success hold you back.

As noted in Chapter 2, "The Reasons Are Within You," the companion fear to Fear of Failure is Fear of Success. As strange as it may sound, a book author might fear success because of preconceived notions about what success will mean, such as, "If this book is successful, will I be able to top it with my next book," or if someone has an approach-avoidance to attention, "If this book takes off, will I have to commit to spending time to promote it that I prefer to put into my family or other responsibilities?"

Although in Chapter 2 you were asked to brainstorm about what success means to you in a general way, take some time to consider what success means to you as it relates to your unfinished manuscript. Perhaps you are writing a memoir, or a true crime nonfiction book, and if your memoir or true crime narrative are successful you may fear those who are mentioned in your memoir, or the subject of your true crime expose, might accuse you of exploiting them. Perhaps you have friends who are book authors and you fear your success might overshadow their careers.

There are no right or wrong success fears; what matters is that you make conscious any anti-success thoughts that are going around in your head that may be stopping you from finishing your book.

18 Improve Your Concentration and Focus So You Get More Done and Finally Finish Your Book.

The *distractionitis* that I discuss throughout this book — letting yourself get pulled away from your priority task by other tasks or even by a text message, checking your e-mail, or answering your cell phone — really takes its toll on finishing up a book. Writing a book requires focus and getting "in the zone" so you can get your book written and rewritten until it is finished. If your concentration is far from optimum, try some of these suggestions, related to writing, and finishing, a book:

1. Start out your day working on your book. Make working on your book your day's first task.
2. Avoid checking e-mails, unless you know that something that is a crisis for your job or personal life needs to be addressed. In that case, you can glance over the e-mails, read the subject line, and decide if you need to open any of the e-mails and read it and/or answer it.
3. Keep your work area uncluttered. If you have lots of pictures and papers posted on your cubicle or in your office, consider removing some or all the items or putting it out of your direct sight.
4. If you feel you are suffering from ADHD (Attention Deficit Hyperactivity Disorder) consider getting help. There are approved drugs that you can take, under medical supervision, to help with your ability to focus if your adult ADHD is impacting on your ability to concentrate.

5. Plan out every day of your week, including your weekend, for optimum efficiency and concentration.
6. Put a sign on your door, if your outside office or home office has a door, "Do not disturb except in emergencies," to help with your concentration and to minimize distractions.
7. If you have trouble concentrating for long periods of time on writing your book, start with a smaller time unit, such as 15 or 30 minutes, or just an hour, and promise yourself you will just write, and avoid all distractions, during that time. As you master being more concentrated, you can increase the amount of time you write, uninterrupted. You may be amazed how quickly this method will help you to get to one, two, or even three hours of uninterrupted writing time without going to the refrigerator for a snack, going online to check your latest e-mail messages, or distracting yourself by reading headlines about celebrity or articles about politics that are completely unrelated to your priority task at hand – finishing up your book.

19 Apply the F-I-N-I-S-H method that you learned about in Chapter 6, "Using the F-I-N-I-S-H," to your goal of finishing up your book manuscript.

F = Focus on your priority task

Put that unfinished book at the top of your pile of things to do. Not buried underneath everything else or hidden away on the shelf or in your drawer. Put whatever draft you have already right on the top of your desk, where you can see it. If someone asks what you're doing you can say, "I'm working on my new book," or "I'm working on an important project." Or just make the time in the morning, after work, or on weekends if you have another job besides writing this book.

I = Ignore interruptions or distractions

Block out time to write your book. That is your book-writing time. Avoid letting anything interrupt you whether those interruptions are self-made or imposed by others. Take control of your time and keep putting this book manuscript first and it will get finished!

N = Now is the time, not later or tomorrow

The time for excuses is over. Put the time and effort into finishing this manuscript, once and for all (until it's published and perhaps down the road you must do an update, if it's nonfiction)!

I = Innovate and initiate so you get this one task done

You may have to be ingenious to find ways to get this book finished. If you work fulltime, you may have to speak into your smartphone, so you record your book-related thoughts. You may have to work on your book during your lunch hour. Without being sleep deprived, you may have to set your alarm an hour earlier or go to bed an hour later. You may have to delegate some of the mundane tasks to an assistant. You will find a way to finish this book if you keep "finish my book" as the priority that it must be.

S = Stay the course till completion, however tough it seems or hard it is to avoid switching tasks

Have a trip coming up? If it is not a business trip you cannot get out of, or a cruise that you paid for that you cannot get a refund, consider postponing all distractions till you finish the book. It is so hard to keep going with a book if you put it aside. Once you get into the book, it is so much easier to get "on a roll" and to keep going with your research and writing (and your rewriting and editing and rewriting). So, keep going and let yourself let the process of finishing take over. You've let the process of delays and not finishing take charge of your mind and your time long enough. Now it is time to keep putting into practice the positive and winning strategies of those who DO finish what they start, including books!

H = Have a "I'm finished!" celebration to applaud your success as you tackle the next priority on your "to do" list.

Start by doing a little dance in your home office or outside office, or just stand up and jump up and down! What can you do to reward yourself for finishing? How about a spontaneous weekend trip or even a night out for dinner and a movie especially if you've put off having fun because you were on a roll with your manuscript. If you are active on social media, you can announce to your Twitter followers, your Facebook fans, or your LinkedIn connections, that you are finished writing your new book. You are sharing not because you are being manipulative and hoping something opportunistic will come from the announcement. You are just sharing because you want to share the sheer joy of being finished. Finishing is joyful especially for a task that may have consumed you for days, weeks, months, years, or even decades.

20 **Positive image yourself finishing your book.**

See yourself finishing your book and opening the envelope with that first physical copy! Envision yourself having a launch party for your book or having it on the New York Times bestseller list. To concretize this last image, get a copy of the *New York Times* bestseller list in your genre. Cut and paste your book at the top of that list!

So, enjoy finishing your book! I will not say "good luck"

finishing your book because you are doing things to make this happen. You are not relying on luck.

Whether it's your first book, your second, or your forty-second, finishing a book takes commitment, courage, and dedication. I am reminded of that adage, "No guts, no glory." Those wise words are true when applied to the monumental task of finishing a book.

21 Treat every book you must write as if it is your first one.

Whether this is your first or your 46th book, if you approach this book with the enthusiasm, wonder, and excitement that most authors bring to that first project, you are more likely to finish what you are working on. Exploit that new author wonder if this is your first book project. If this is another book for you to finish, forget about all the positive or negatives associated with those other finished books. Instead, see this as a self-contained book that you want to write — that you need to write and finish —as well as to take the important next step, getting it published, whether you turn the book over to a commercial or academic house or self-publish it. Congratulate yourself for a job well done!

Whether it is your first book, your fifth, or your 50th, finishing a book takes a commitment to that task and an attitude, as well as actions, that make that monumental task the focus of your time. If you work fulltime, besides writing, you may have to budget time during lunch, before or after work, or on weekends, to finish your book, but you can make it happen.

EXERCISES

1. I remember when I shared with a noted sociologist that I had finally finished my dissertation. He wrote back that one of the benefits of finishing it is that I would not have to

keep explaining why I was not finished yet! Sounds simple enough, but anyone who has ever tried to, or succeeded at, working on a book length project, like a dissertation or a more popular book or novel, knows that it is something that takes a lot of drive, stick-to-it-ive-ness, and commitment to make that book happen. To help you to keep yourself motivated, check off all the reasons you want to finish this book. If your reasons are missing from the list, add those reasons in where it says "other."

Making money	Curiosity about what the process is like
Sharing what I have to say	Curiosity about what it is like to be a book author
Changing the world	Enhancing my image as an expert
Entertaining others	Aiding my career
The process of writing is rewarding	Helping others
Branding	Other ________________
International recognition	Other ________________
Achieving a goal, I have set for myself	Other ________________
Educating others	Other ________________
Fulfilling a professional commitment	

2. Sometimes it is useful to remind yourself how important books have been in your lifetime as a motivator to keep writing your own book until it is finished and published. Use the space below to write down the books and/or authors

who have most influenced you throughout your lifetime. Just write down the top one or, at the most, the top three in each category. If you have not read a book in a category, or if you do not remember the titles, or nothing you read was especially memorable, just leave it blank.

Children's picture books

____

____

____

Middle school books

____

____

____

Young adult books

____

____

____

Adult nonfiction

____

____

____

Adult fiction

____

____

____

Memoirs

____

____

____

Poetry

____

____

____

3. In the last exercise you wrote down one or up to three books in a variety of categories over your lifetime that have been memorable or important to you. Now write down your own book in the space below. See it published and see it on the list of memorable books that someone else is putting together, perhaps even in their copy of this book!

    I will write this idea down in the form of an affirmation as a way of reinforcing, and motivating, you to finish your book:

    I am the author of a new book that others are finding memorable.

    The book is called ______________________________.

Fill in the title of your book!

PART 3: FURTHER THOUGHTS AND A CONCLUSION

CHAPTER 12

The Exception That Proves the Rule: When Failing to Finish Is a Good Thing

The overriding theme of this book so far has been how to help you finish everything that you start especially if you have one or many unfinished tasks or projects, whether it is redecorating your home, finishing college, or turning in the blog that is due by the end of the day. In this chapter we will explore the more philosophical idea of deciding just what you should be finishing in the first place. When is putting something aside a good decision, that is conscious and based on assessing the situation and deciding that not finishing is the best thing to do versus failing to finish because of unresolved unconscious issues or bad habits like fear or failure, fear of success, procrastination, insecurity, or devaluing your abilities?

Failing to Finish for All the Right Reasons

To some extent I touched on this concept in Chapter 7, "Taking Control: Goal Setting and Prioritizing," but this is such a pivotal issue in getting a grip on your finishing challenges that I want to address it again. That is because finishing is really part of the broader question, "Should I have started this in the first place?"

If your answer is, "No," then it is okay to leave it unfinished, whatever it is.

There are some tasks, projects, and even relationships, that now, under reconsideration, you should not have initiated. When you make those considered judgments, then deciding not to finish is a good thing, not a sign of failure or defeat.

None of us are stagnant. Although, in general, our values remain somewhat consistent over time, there are ideas or considerations that lead us to decide that our energy and talent is better placed in another direction. I want to use my own art career as an example of this. I majored in fine art in college and I even had a one-person art show at the National Arts Club when I was 28. I instead pursued a career in publishing and writing, as well as criminal justice and, later, as a sociologist and academic.

Although over the years I have used my own art work for covers and even in the interior of many books, but I always wondered if maybe I should have kept trying to have a career as a professional artist. I knew trying to be a fulltime artist was going to be a very long, tough road and I made the other choices since I could only put my energy into so many avenues and still have time for my husband and raising our two sons, who are now grown.

A year ago, I joined the Stamford Artists Association and took one of the two available one-person show slots that they make available to members each year. I was so excited by my first show in decades, putting together dozens of my available works and even getting written up in the local newspaper.

The show was well attended, and I even sold half a dozen collages and paintings.

Ironically, this second show confirmed that I had made the right decision to pursue the other careers that I had chosen, rather than becoming a fulltime artist. This second show helped me to feel less like a quitter.

I also learned about an online galley, Saatchiart.com, which displays my original works that are for sale so I feel a little less guilty about my career choices.

So, I ask you to consider one or more of the projects that you feel you want to finish and to assess if it is something that you really want to do —or must do —or if there are very logical, noteworthy reasons that it should be put aside, temporarily or even permanently.

You want to make an active decision, based on weighing the pros and cons of a situation or a project, making your decision about whether to keep going forward or to put it aside, based on clear thoughts rather than out of frustration, depression, or feeling temporarily defeated.

Let's say that you want to get a Fulbright Scholarship to teach in Denmark for two weeks next summer. But you decide that you have a better offer and you cannot pursue both opportunities. That is a very different scenario than if you fail to go to Denmark on a Fulbright because you left your application unfinished and therefore did not get it in by the deadline, so you could even be considered.

I am reminded of a pro-active decision to change courses in his life that Charles Krauthammer, the late syndicated American political columnist. He became a Harvard-trained psychiatrist. Even becoming paralyzed from the neck down in a diving accident could not stop him from graduating from medical school. But over time, as he said in many of the interviews that were broadcast upon his death from cancer at the age of 67 in June 2018, he decided that writing and broadcast journalism called to him. He gave up psychiatry becoming a commentator for Fox News, among other jobs, and he never looked back.

Adam Hergenrother, founder and CEO of five companies, now shares about the benefits of deciding to quit other projects or ventures: As Hergenrother notes, "I'm not advocating quitting or for not pushing through in the face of fear or failure - that is critical to any successful journey - but what I am saying is that it is okay to realize that the path you started down is no longer the path you want to be on. Adjusting your course is a part of life."

Dr. Marlene Caroselli, who has published 62 books, including *Defeating Procrastination*, echoes Hergenrother's view. Notes Dr. Caroselli, "Finishing everything we have started could evince obsessive behavior. It's better to leave projects that we discover will not have the return on investment we initially anticipate. Moderation in all things, the ancient Greeks advised."

Remember Pareto's 80/20 rule that we explored in Chapter 7 on goal setting and prioritizing? That concept got applied to other situations and, over time, it has come to mean that 20 percent of your efforts will get you 80 percent of your results. If you apply that to the concept of finishing, you just might be better off figuring out what the 80 percent payoff will be and selectively zoning in on that 20 percent effort.

As stated at the beginning of this book, one of my goals is to help you to make more active and conscious decisions about what to finish rather than falling into the unfinished trap out of any of the 22 behaviors, beliefs, or bad habits that we explored in Chapter 2 especially doing too much as once, fear of failure, perfectionism, procrastination, lacking a deadline, or having an unrealistic one, interrupting yourself before you are done and switching to another project, or anger, for starters.

The Hemingway Effect

I found an interesting study conducted in Japan that set out to prove something that the researchers, Yoshinori Oyama, Emmanuel Manalo, and Yoshihide Nakatani, refer to as the Hemingway effect. In the corrected proof of their research findings, posted online under the title, "The Hemingway effect: How failing to finish a task can have a positive effect on motivation," they conclude that "Motivation to persist in a failed-to-finish task is related to completion closeness."

Why do they call this phenomenon that they discovered the Hemingway Effect? It is based on the quote from an interview with the famous writer Ernest Hemingway who answered the question, "How much should you write in a day?" in this way, "The best way is always to stop when you are going good and when you know what will happen next. If you do that every day when you are writing a novel you will never be stuck."

To test out Hemingway's advice, the researchers had 260 first year undergraduate students at a university in Japan perform a newspaper copying task in two groups. The students were told to stop copying after 2 minutes and 40 seconds so that the majority had failed to finish the assigned task. The students were then asked to count and calculate the number of remaining text characters that they had failed to copy.

What were the results? The researchers feel that they confirmed the presence of what they have termed the Hemingway Effect in that "the fewer script characters they were not able to finish copying, the more motivated they reported wanting to continue the task to finish it."

How does this apply to your finishing challenges? If the researchers are correct, it means that if you can somehow force yourself to get closer to completion of a task, rather than just totally abandon it, your drive to pick up that task again, and take it to completion will be enhanced.

In a second study to test out the Hemingway Effect, 131 undergraduates were given a short writing task. The task was divided into two types: structured or unstructured. Once again, the groups were interrupted so they could not finish the requested task. What was so interesting in the findings of this second study is that only the participants who were given the structured task showed signs of the Hemingway Effect. What that means for you and I is that the more specific we are in what remains to be done in an unfinished task, the more likely we are to be motivated to return to it, and to finish it.

Having an unfinished task that is too unstructured or open ended does not have the same "pull" to complete it. This phenomenon is an outgrowth of the research studies done by Maria Ovsiankina in 1928 and Bluma Zeigarnik in 1927. Their experiments concluded that if participants were interrupted before completing a task, Zeigarnik found that the study participants had better recall of the tasks that were unfinished. Ovsiankina discovered that participants would resume tasks and complete those tasks even if there was no material benefit to them. Oayma et. al. concludes, "…task performance interruption does tend to make people want to later re-engage in the unfinished task – or even a substitute – in an apparent need for some form of closure."

What these studies imply is that having an unfinished project, especially if it is close to finishing, may not be all that negative. There is a drive to finish it especially "if they think they were close to finishing."

So being positive about the prospects of completing a task or project may be a key element in applying this research to your own work and personal life so you get more done. Instead of totally abandoning a project because it remains unfinished and you feel disheartened that you will ever get it done, see the incomplete status as a motivator.

EXERCISES

1. As an extension of the so-called Hemingway Effect described in this chapter, write down a list of "almost finished" projects that you have. If you are trying to decide what project to finish next, perhaps you might be more motivated if you choose from this "almost finished" list rather than projects that have a much longer way to go. (This assumes that everything else is equal and that you can select which projects to finish. In many work settings, however, you will be told by your boss, or a schedule that you have agreed to, what you must do next.)

   List of almost finished tasks or projects

   1. ________________________________

   2. ________________________________

3. ____

4. ____

5. ____

2. Go back to the first chapter in this book where you made a very lengthy "to do" list. Reconsider what is on that list from the very minor to the major tasks or projects. Are there now things you thought you had to finish that, based on what you have learned about yourself in this book, that you feel it is okay to quit or abandon? Remember, you want to stop working on something because you consciously decide that it is in your best interest to temporarily or permanently delay finishing something. You are not letting some of the unconscious pulls, like fear or failure or fear of success, or bad habits, like procrastination or perfectionism, stop you from finishing.

   Revise your original list, as needed, pruning down what you must finish or, in some instances, even adding to that list priority concerns that you were unaware that you even needed to pursue.

CHAPTER 13

Concluding Thoughts

Wow, even those words, "Concluding Thoughts," feel good to write. Those words mean that I am close to the end of this book. It is a bittersweet feeling. As challenging as it was to finally put aside all other distractions and throw myself into the process of writing this book, after getting a commitment to it from my publisher in India six months ago based on a detailed outline and sample chapter, once I got into researching and writing it, I found myself enjoying the process. When you begin a new semester as a college professor, students and professors alike are mindful of when the course will end, looking forward to that ending. But when that day arrives, most are ambivalent about the ending. Students are even ambivalent about graduating, after four or five years, and moving on to the next step in their lives.

Facing how most of us have mixed feelings about finishing can free you up to finish more often. You cannot deal with that confusing mixed feeling unless you finish! By failing to finish, you are in a state of limbo which, in most cases, is far worse than the nostalgic feeling that finishing usually brings with it.

What is the cure for that nostalgic or ambivalent feeling when you finish? Once you have taken some time out to celebrate the victory of finishing, it is best to throw yourself into the next task or project. You want to keep moving forward, to new challenges, activities, and unfinished undertakings that you want to complete.

Thanks for reading this book and doing the exercises at the end of each chapter. As with all self-help books, the more effort you put into it, the more likely you are to see some positive behavioral changes although, there are no guarantees.

Before we turn to how your life might look if you get more finished and OTD – Out the Door – I want to share a secret with you. Although writing down your goals may help to concretize those goals, as well as making to-do lists that help keep you on track, but sometimes telling others about your unfinished projects can backfire. Or, when you finally do pick up something that you have been working on for a long time, you may be surprised that those closest to you, rather than cheering you on, express boredom at hearing about that project "yet again."

So be careful who you share with about your unfinished projects. Writing things down so you make yourself more accountable to yourself should be useful and if you have supportive friends, family, or colleagues with whom you can share about your unfinished tasks or projects, that is great. But sometimes you must keep what you have put aside a secret so that you are not unnecessarily discouraged. You can announce the news that you are finally finished when the time comes and what a great feeling that will be!

The Hawthorne Effect

The Hemingway Effect discussed in the last chapter, namely, that the closer you are to finishing something, the greater the pull to finish, made me think of the Hawthorne Effect since it ties in with what I just mentioned to you, about the benefits of keeping your goals secret. The early research in factories and productivity that led to what we call The Hawthorne Effect is actually almost the opposite of keeping your goals, or specific project that you need to finish, secret that I just mentioned. The Hawthorne Effect was the term given to the phenomenon that occurred when workers were assessed as to whether they were more or less productive based on the amount of light on their work. The time and place of the research site was Hawthorne Works, a Western Electric factory located outside of Chicago, between 1924 and 1932. Initially it was the amount of light that was considered the cause of the increase in productivity. Later, it was decided that it was the act of observing the workers that led to their increased productivity, rather than the light.

How does this pertain to finishing? By telling someone about your efforts to finish something, and having that person cheer you on, you might actually help yourself to be more productive. Be careful, however, whom you choose to be your mentor or advocate. If you pick someone who makes you feel guilty about how long you are taking, or who questions if you are not taking enough time if your work is a quality effort, you may not have the desired Hawthorne Effect of increased productivity.

Paperwork

The bulk of this book has been addressing the "big" tasks or projects, the major activities that could make or break your career. But for many of us, how we handle such everyday "little" things like paperwork, or filing, and answering e-mails or calls, or placing them, are issues that need to be addressed in a book about finishing. It is sometimes how you handle the little things, like paperwork, that can determine how fast, easily, or even if you ever get to finish the bigger tasks. I know this goes against the grain of the mega-bestseller, *Don't Sweat the Small Stuff*, but sometimes it is the small stuff that looms large and the big stuff that you can reduce to smaller pieces that becomes much more minor.

I know having a paperless office has for many, including me, been the goal for a long time, especially since computers replaced typewriters. Also, with the advent of Cloud storage, including such services as Dropbox or Microsoft's OneDrive, storing backups of your electronic materials is easier than ever. Printing out on paper, creating the clutter that then must be filed, is optional.

At least I always think it is until I cannot find a file on my hard drive, or on my back-up travel drives or in my Cloud storage, and I am so grateful that I did print out a physical copy that was filed.

You must decide how you will handle your paperwork but the key point about paperwork in a book on finishing, even if the paperwork is electronically-stored files, is that you need to attend to it. If you fail to finish filing papers related to the project that you are working on, or to save your important electronic files to one or more alternative places in case the hard drive of your main computer gets wiped out and cannot be restored, you will be extremely upset. Depending upon what you lose, or misplace, your work may be set back hours, days, weeks, or even years.

Creating a system for dealing with your paperwork, a way of handling paper or electronic files, that works for you is essential. There is no one way to do it. There are those who like the online commercial programs that offer to organize your data or files for you. If that works for you, great.

Try to have a naming standard with your electronic files so it is easier to locate things later. Back-up, back-up, back-up is advice that you need to heed since there are untold ways that files can get misplaced or wiped out, especially if you lack a paper version of it.

I even send important files to myself, so I have some type of copy of it that I could track down, if need be.

Dealing with E-mails, Texts, or Calls

Another part of the unfinished epidemic that I have observed is those who fail to return a phone call, respond to a text, or reply to an e-mail. There is a dance that two party participate in when they communicate with each other. Answering a text, returning a phone call, or replying to an e-mail is part of that dance. Although sometimes it is okay not to respond — yes, there are times when a communication is self-contained, and no answer is implied or necessary — but most of the time, a reaction in the form of a comeback is required and expected.

By answering the e-mail, by returning the phone call if you got a voice mail, or by responding to a text, you are finishing the two-way communication in a positive way. You can mix and match it up. You can e-mail in response to a voicemail or call as your answer to a text. But there usually needs to be some type of reaction to the other party's communication or the exchange feels unfinished.

Since we have been discussing such "big" concerns in this book, from finishing a book to planning an annual corporate retreat, responding to each phone call, text, or e-mail seems, at first glance, to be such a minor concern. But in too many cases, those unfinished communications can grow into misunderstandings, feelings of abandonment, faded friendships, or weakened business associations.

Another version of this is when people get together at a conference or in a business meeting and promises are made to follow-up on a meeting. One or both parties may or may not follow-up. If there is no follow-up, the promises that were made at the meeting are unfinished. The interaction that started with so much promise and enthusiasm may probably now faulter or flounder. Without finishing up what was decided upon at the initial meeting, if nothing ensues from that first contact, the whole thing may be deemed a waste of time. Not only is a second meeting unlikely, but you risk getting a reputation for failing to follow-up or being "more talk than action."

Years ago, I went to a workshop on subsidiary and foreign rights. Even though I do subsidiary and foreign rights, and I even offer workshops myself, I find it interesting, on occasion, to see what others are teaching and sharing. One of the attendees shared with the room of rights managers and publishers his frustration that every time he attended a book fair and had lots of meetings, he had to follow-up on those meetings. He had a huge stack of requests that he had to follow-up on and he had been putting it off. It was going to be so many hours of work! He was dismayed by the challenge of it!

There is no easy answer for him. An obvious one is for him to consider delegating the follow-up to someone else at his company. From his comments, however, he seemed to be the one to whom all the follow-up had fallen.

So, what's the solution? Complaining might be cathartic but putting in the time and effort, one by one taking care of each request, is the way he will finish going through that huge stack of requests. Maybe he could train an intern for credit to help him although he would have to factor in the time and effort to train someone and then the necessary supervision and review of his/her work.

He might investigate specialized software or other technological tools to facilitate his follow-up. Whether he does it manually, or he finds a more systematic electronic or technological way to accomplish his follow-up, what is essential is that he does it. Ignoring the pile will have consequences.

Sometimes things are unfinished because circumstances change. I recently wrote to someone who was handling something for me at a company in India. It had been more than a month since that individual was supposed to complete the task at hand. I got an autoresponder advising me that the individual had left the company. Fortunately, they provided the name and e-mail address of an alternative person to communicate with. But it would have been so much nicer if the employee who was leaving had sent me that information pro-actively. It would have saved me the five weeks of lost time resolving the issue that I now was facing.

What Could Your Life Be Like If You Selectively Finished Everything You Started?

How about considering the psychological benefits of finishing? Here are just some of the responses to my question to 205 men and women, "What could your life be like if you selectively finished everything that you started?"

"Everything will be great"

"Less stressful"

"Wonderful"

"My life really will be better"

"It would be easier and less cluttered."

"More organized, less chaotic."

Only five out of 205 thought that finishing everything you start would be a negative thing. They described the result in this way:

Boring (4)

Predictable (1)

We do not know how those five individual's unfinished projects are impacting on others who may be waiting on their incomplete tasks. But unless those five individuals change their attitude about finishing – seeing it as a positive thing rather than something potentially negative – I will just have to focus on helping the 200 people who do think selectively finishing everything you start will make life less stressful, "amazing," and "wonderful."

So, write down what word you would use to describe how you will feel if you finish everything you start. That concept might help you to understand that procrastination is stopping you from having that positive new feeling.

____

If you're in a safe situation, close your eyes and imagine yourself handing everything in on time that you have due, getting out from under the feeling of being overwhelmed by incomplete tasks, from sending out new product announcement e-mails or cards to updating your smartphone, that take up so much of your energy.

There are some people who are just better at doing things till completion. I asked a business writer for a major corporation who has that ability and he replied, "No tricks to share. Just ass to chair till I get it done."

But what if you would like to be like that but you seem to get too distracted and to start, and stop, too many tasks or projects that remain unfinished? What could you do to turn things around? You might just need to consider getting professional help.

Getting Help

ADHD

The advice in this book is for informational purposes only and it is very general comments about why projects are unfinished, what might cause it, and how to finish more often. But although I am a sociologist and I did graduate work in psychiatric art therapy, I am not a medical doctor.

For some, there might be medical reasons that projects are unfinished such as if you or your teen have undiagnosed ADHD which stands for attention deficit hyperactivity disorder.

Only a physician or an expert in ADHD can diagnose if you have ADHD or not but if you have a chronic problem with finishing projects, you might want to rule out if there is a physical or neurological reason behind it and, based on what you discover in an evaluation, if medication is recommended to help your condition. The National Institute of Mental Health (NIMH) outlines some of the key symptoms of ADHD, a brain disorder, in their online fact sheet, "Attention Deficit Hyperactivity Disorder." Of the three key symptoms – inattention, hyperactivity, and impulsivity, inattention seems closest to the tendency to leave projects unfinished syndrome. As the NIMH notes, "Inattention means a person wanders off task, lacks persistence, has difficulty sustaining focus, and is disorganized; and these problems are not due to defiance or lack of comprehension."

As with finding any physician or mental health specialist to help you, start with friends and family members who may have recommended a physician or mental health specialist, such as a psychologist or counselor, or clinical social worker with expertise in ADHD that you could meet with for an evaluation. Do your online, book, and article research but that should not substitute for a medical evaluation. If necessary, based on the first evaluation that you receive, consider getting a second evaluation.

Terry Matlen is a clinical social worker, and author of *The Queen of Distraction*, who consults on ADHD, a condition she deals with herself. Matlen shared how ADHD makes it harder for those who have it to finish things:

> *Adults with ADHD struggle with finishing (and starting) projects because of difficulties in our executive function, which is the part of the brain that, in simple terms, helps us figure out how to get from A to B. This creates a tremendous amount of anxiety, even to the point of clinical depression, because it can affect all areas of life: keeping our homes tidy, planning meals, getting projects done at work on time. This takes a toll – a deep toll – on adults with ADHD, affecting self-esteem, relationships, and more. The symptoms of ADHD are typically inattention, hyperactivity/impulsivity, and more, yet many – especially women—struggle more with inattention. We get thrown off course very easily due to distractability, thus starting a project often leads to not finishing a project because we notice other things that need our attention. And off we go, totally off course.*

Some other reasons for those with ADHD failing to finish? Matlen continues:

> *Another part of it, for me, is procrastination due to a number of things: feeling overwhelmed with all the things needed to do and therefore just not doing them; having issues with executive functioning, as mentioned before, that makes it hard to know where to start and how to finish; and a fear of boredom. Ask anyone with ADD what one of the worst sensations to have and many will say, "Not being able to tolerate boredom." It plays out in so many ways. For example, we are often very impatient.*

As noted at the beginning of this section on ADHD, and earlier in the book, a diagnosis of ADHD needs to be made by a physician or mental health practitioners who are experienced with ADHD, such as psychologists or counselors, who could make the proper diagnosis. As a separate issue from that diagnosis, I refer you back to Chapter 2 where you will find under Fear of Completion the suggestion that if you have another project lined up to follow the one you want to finish first, that could help you cope with the fear of boredom that might underly your reluctance to finish.

In his intriguing reprinted article from the *Harvard Business Review*, "Overloaded Circuits," Edward M. Hallowell writes about ADT which he refers to as attention deficit trait. He says this is "caused by brain overload, ADT is now epidemic in organizations. The core symptoms are distractibility, inner frenzy, and impatience." Hallowell continues, listing the consequences of ADT: "People with ADT have difficult staying organized, setting priorities, and managing time." I would add that those suffering from ADT are more likely to have unfinished tasks or projects.

What does Hallowell suggest as a way of managing ADT in the workplace? His first suggestion is to promote positive emotions. Working around people, rather than in physical isolation, helps. He has a very clear suggestion in this regard, "When you make time at least every four to six hours for a 'human moment,' a face-to-face exchange with a person you like, you are giving your brain what it needs."

His next suggestion is "Take physical care of your brain." Hallowell says that you can achieve that by getting enough sleep, exercising, and have a good diet, all sound advice.

He also suggests being more organized so that you attend to the more important tasks at the beginning of the day, rather than just dealing with e-mail, followed by "protect your frontal lobes." He notes you can do that by heeding this advice: "slow down."

In the Resources section you will find listings for ADHD-related associations, for more information. Working with a professional organizer may help someone with ADHD to increase their success rate at finishing projects. In the Resources section you will find a listing for NAPO, National Organization of Productivity and Organizing Professionals, which maintains a directory of members available for in-person or phone coaching or even more "hands on" direct assistance.

Working with a Project Manager

Project managers are another consideration if you are working on one or multiple projects and the complexities of those tasks is beyond your organizational skills. Asking for help from a project manager might be a positive step rather than a sign of defeat. If you are stalled on a task or project, and failing to finish it, it might be because you need help with all the myriad of tasks that will go into completing that task. What are some of the benefits of working with a project manager? Since they are responsible for the planning, budgeting, and monitoring of a project, it could be a way to keep you on track, providing you with interim deadlines and having someone to whom you are accountable, so you are less likely to fall behind.

You need to know if you or your company have any project managers on staff that might be available to you or if you have the budget to hire a project manager as a consultant. If you or your company decide to green light the idea of having a project manager work with you, you want to do your due diligence in screening one or more applicants for this job. Especially if you are dealing with a very complex project, you may be working together for days, weeks, months, or, in some instances, even years. You need to respect and get along with each other and you also need to feel that the way that he or she works will be in sync with your personality and sensibilities. You might want to give one or more potential project managers a sample piece of the project, or another hypothetical project, to work up so you can see that person in action as well as to gauge your interaction.

"If you have a big thing you're working on, it's really smart to think in terms of working with a project manager," says Lisa Vento Nielsen, a Staten Island, New York-based project manager who runs two small businesses and is also a certified PMP (Project Management Professional). Nielsen agrees that entrepreneurs who have the tendency to try to do everything themselves may especially benefit from delegating the planning of an entire project to a project manager or just working with a project manager to get through their to do list. "A lot of times they just need a little bit of insight and a little bit of prioritization," says Nielsen. "They have hundreds of things on their to do list. What should they do first?"

If you cannot afford a project manager, Nielsen suggests considering bartering your services if you have something to offer the project manager in exchange.

When You are Not the Problem

Maybe occasionally you have something that needs to be finished, but, overall, this is really the problem of those who work for you.

You are, after all, the CEO or head of the whole company. You probably would not have gotten to run the company if you left too many things unfinished.

A CEO in Sweden, who considers himself very efficient, and although he works hard, he does not see himself as a workaholic, shares that his biggest time challenge is "motivating a team that is easily distracted to stick to one task at a time *and finish it*." [I added the italics for emphasis!]

So, what can you do if you find yourself in that situation? Here are some suggestions to motivate your team to prioritize and focus:

1. Create a handout of readings of books on getting things finished. (For your convenience, I have created such a list in the appendix.)
2. Select one book from that list and buy copies of the book for your entire staff.
3. Together, read and discuss the book. Have a workshop related to that book that you conduct or bring in an outside trainer. If possible, serve lunch or refreshments.
4. Consider creating a better reward system for those who get more efficient at finishing. You might offer a cash bonus, a gift card for merchandise or a favorite restaurant.
5. Set up regular meetings individually with each employee who has a finishing challenge. Work with them on the underlying causes, how they will work on these issues, and their plan for getting better at finishing.
6. Consider implementing a daily routine like the one that David Niu, Founder and CEO at TINYpulse, headquartered in Seattle with a branch in Vietnam, does at his company. As Niu explains: "The whole company gathers every morning for a stand-up meeting

for a quick status update on what they have done the previous day (a green check or a red cross) or any blocking issues that need to be prioritized. During the standup meeting, I can understand what blocks my team from achieving their end goal or what they have been working on so I can jump in and give my feedback to help him or her to finish their work. By stating the number one roadblock during the standup meeting, other teams will notice and if they have great resources or solutions, they will be able to share and support each other after the meeting."

Top 7 Tips to Finishing Everything You Start

There is a world of distractions, competing demands on your work and personal time, cell phones ringing, electronic devices reminding you of everything from when to wake up to someone's upcoming birthday or anniversary. What are you to do to cut through all that noise and get your priority projects done or to make your way down your to-do list of big and small responsibilities that you are determined not to let fall through the cracks?

Here are my top 7 tips to finishing everything you start. Some are more extreme than others. Remember just because a suggestion works for me, or selectively works for others, does not mean this is your best option. But consider one or more of these strategies especially if lately your productivity and focus is poorer than usual:

1. Be ruthless about focusing in on what you deem your number 1 priority project or task to do. Say "no" to everyone and anyone who interferes with your commitment to finishing it.
2. If you are completely distracted by all the competing demands on your time, take the #1 thing you must do

and, if necessary, go to another location —in your office building, in your home, outside of your office or home, if necessary — and focus on doing it.

3. Remind yourself that whatever it is that you are putting off finishing is worth completing because there are consequences to things that are left in an unfinished status.
4. Repeat the affirmation, "I am finishing what I started."
5. Strive for achievable excellence rather than unattainable perfection that can stop you from finishing.
6. Although starting is important since that's the first step in finishing anything, most people find finishing more challenging, so you are not alone if finishing is hard for you.
7. Go back to the F-I-N-I-S-H acronym to spur yourself on:

   F = Focus on one priority task.

   I = Ignore interruptions or distractions.

   N = Now is the time, not later or tomorrow.

   I = Initiate and innovate so you keep going.

   S = Stay the course however tough it gets.

   H = Hail finishing by celebrating your accomplishment.

A caveat about the above tips: Use your judgment when or if to apply any of the above strategies. Use your judgment about the ruthless part. If a dependent child or needy friend asks for your attention, put aside what you are focusing on but get back to it as soon as possible.

Stay positive and keep reminding yourself and forcing

yourself to do the actions that will back that affirmation up, that you are finishing what in your good judgment you want to finish.

Remind yourself that you can finish. After all, you have done it many times before. Now apply those positive steps to this project or task because we are judged by what we are doing now and tomorrow. Yesterday counts but it is important to keep moving forward.

In considering #7, F-I-N-I-S-H, discussed in Chapter 6 and reviewed above, you can empower yourself to improve your productivity even more by following the D-O I-T N-O-W acronym that I created in my *Creative Time Management for the New Millennium*. Those concepts are still valid. (See each one described in the Appendix in "The 7 Principles of Creative Time Management.")

Know Thyself

Understanding yourself better, how you work best, whether or not you can handle distractions, what happens to your body, and your mind, if you fail to take adequate breaks, are all issues that will help you, and your staff, deal with the challenging of finish everything you start.

What are your energy highs and lows? Are you a morning or an evening person? Perhaps you are up and working by four in the morning, but you find yourself feeling somewhat tired by five or six o'clock? There is no right or wrong to being a morning or evening person. As one Colorado-based consultant put it, "I'm a morning person so I work best in the morning." He maximizes the benefit of being a morning person in how he schedules his time at work: "I get into work early and there aren't as many people around to distract me."

All that matters is that you know yourself, and those who

work for you know themselves, so you can make that self-knowledge work for you.

We all want to accomplish each day what really matters and, in a week, a month, a year, and even in a lifetime, we want to finish what is important to us professionally and personally.

Prioritizing is key. What is the most important project or task to do —to finish — *now*?

There are also some projects that are just so big or that are going to take you in a completely different direction than the one you are going in now that you may take quite a while to finish it. Some of those concerns may be activities that you put on what has come to be known as the "Bucket List," the list of things you want to do before you die. But you can call that list of yours anything you like if you prefer a title that is less of a reminder of our mortality, such as My Dream List or My Wish List. I know what is on my Wish List: Get a movie made and get a play produced. I need to break up those huge tasks into more manageable steps. But since so much of my energy these days is focused on writing books, coaching, teaching college courses, and helping other authors by ghostwriting, consulting, or selling foreign rights, I just have to keep reminding myself of those goals so I make both goals happen when it is possible to make the time.

As my friend, the late actor and author David Carradine, wrote to me in an e-mail "There are no failures in Hollywood. Only people who give up too soon."

So, it is okay if you have unfinished projects or other concerns that you have on your own wish list. Write down those big dreams and keep reminding yourself about those goals until you can make the time to finish those objectives. Whether it takes a week, a month, a year, or a lifetime, making your aspirations come true is what it is all about. Use the space below to commit to writing your professional or personal Wish List:

My Wish List

Today's date: ______________________

Professional wish list

1. ____
2. ____
3. ____

Personal wish list

4. ____
5. ____
6. ____

I hope *How to Finish Everything You Start* has empowered you to make better choices about what to finish and, if you do let something go by the wayside, not to feel as guilty about it. Whether it's a business association you have decided it is time to move on from, or a task at work that you shelved because a more important project landed on your lap, sometimes it simply is okay to let people or things go.

As Xavier Parkhouse-Parker, Co-Founder of ZapHub, a marketing company based in the United Kingdom, wrote, in answer to my question, "When is it okay to not finish a task or project?" "When it's not important anymore" adding to his comment that, for him, "the only things that don't get finished are things that didn't need doing."

Hopefully you have discovered that knowing if you find it easier to start, rather than finish, a project helps you to know yourself better so you are more aware of where you need to put more of your energy. The goal of *How to Finish Everything You Start* is for you to finish those projects, or to pursue those relationships, that you do want to continue or finish without letting a fear of completion, procrastination, or any of the other reasons we have explored stop you.

So, we have come to the end of *How to Finish Everything Your Start*. Thank you for taking this journey with me! In the back matter you will find the Selected Bibliography Including Cited Works, Resources, Appendix, and About the Author. In the About the Author, you will find my website and e-mail address listed for follow-up. I hope this information is contributing to you finishing more projects at work, getting more books written, reaching the goal in your weight loss program, cleaning up your clutter, returning to college or graduate school to finish up your degree, or whatever additional work or business goals you have that were incomplete.

EXERCISES

1. What is your #1 takeaway or key idea from this book? Write it down.

   ____

2. Perhaps you are not the one with the finishing challenge or you feel you now have a better grip on this tendency. What if someone you care about, or someone you work with, leaves things unfinished. How will you handle helping him or her to get more done although being a role model and setting a positive example will help?

   ____

   ____

   ____

3. Thank you, once again, for reading *How to Finish Everything You Start*. In addition to my three other time management books — *Work Less, Do More*; *Creative Time Management for the New Millennium*; and *Put More Time on Your Side*

— in my survey of 205 men and women, these were the top 5 books readers have read on time management, listed in order of popularity. I do have to let you know, however, that I unintentionally left off the list one of the most popular books: *The Life-Changing Magic of Tidying Up* by Marie Kondo. Readers were instructed to include in the "other" section any books they have read that was missing from the list.

The 7 Habits of Highly Effective People by Steven Covey (by far the most popular time management book with almost 16% or 28 readers)

Following Through by *Steven Levinson*

The Power to Get Things Done by Steven Levinson

The Follow-Through by Gene Hayden

The 4-Hour Work Week by Tim Ferriss

Full bibliographic citations are included in the "Selected Bibliography with Lists of Works Cited" in the back of this book. To reinforce what you have learned in *How to Finish Everything You Start*, as well as to open yourself up to additional insights and suggestions that deal with this and other time management issues, I invite you to consider reading the print or e-book version of any of these books, or even to listen to the audiobook as you work out in the gym, take a power walk at lunchtime or during your commute, as long as you are in a safe situation, such as on a train or bus, and not listening to a book while driving and unnecessarily distracting yourself.

Selected Bibliography Including Cited Works

In addition to the complete citation for any works cited in this book, you will find a collection of targeted and more general books or articles on time management as well as making the most of your life. There are numerous time management books available to you so I do not claim that this list is definitive.

Acuff, Jon. *Finish: Give Yourself the Gift of Done* by Jon Acuff. New York: Portfolio (Penguin Random House Company), 2017.

Barkas, J.L. (see Jan Yager) *Creative Time Management* Englewood Cliffs, NJ: Prentice-Hall, 1984.

Blake, Jenny. *Pivot: The Only Move That Matters Is Your Next One.* NY: Portfolio/Penguin Random House, 2016.

Blanchard, Ken and Spencer Johnson. *The One Minute Manager.* NY: William Morrow, 1982.

Canfield, Jack; Mark Victor Hansen; and Les Hewitt. *The Power of Focus.* Deerfield Beach, FL: HCI Communications, 2012.

Carlozo, Lou. "Why college students stop short of a degree." Reuters. March 27, 2012.

Cockerham, William C. *Medical Sociology.* 10th edition. Englewood Cliffs, NJ: Prentice-Hall, 2006.

Corpuz, John. "Best Calendar Apps." Posted on April 23, 2018 at Toms Guide: https://www.tomsguide.com/us/pictures-story/442-best-calendar-apps.html

Covey, Stephen. The 7 *Habits of Highly Effective People.* NY: Simon & Schuster, Inc., 1989.

Davis, Sampson; George Jenkins; and Rameck Hunt with Lisa Frazier Page. *The Pact.* NY: Riverhead Books, 2003.

Dearden, Lizzie. "The books many start but few finish: Top 'unread' bestsellers revealed." July 8, 2014. Published in the UK Independent newspaper online.

Drucker, Peter. *The Daily Drucker*. NY: HarperBusiness, 2004.

Farkas, Dora. "7 Reasons Why Bright Students Drop Out of Grad School" November 4, 2016, Posted at https://finishyourthesis.com/drop-out/

Ferriss, Timothy. *The 4-Hour Workweek.* Timothy Ferriss. Vermillion. 2008. New edition, Crown Publishers, 2007, 2009.

Gazzaley, Adam and Larry D. Rosen. *The Distracted Mind: Ancient Brains in a High-Tech World.* Cambridge, MA: The MIT Press, 2017.

Hansen, Morten T. Great at Work: How Top Performers Do Less, Work Better, and Achieve More. NY: Simon & Schuster, Inc., 2018.

Hallowell, Edward M. "Overloaded Circuits: Why Smart People Underperform." Harvard Business Review on Managing Yourself. Boston, MA: Harvard Business School Press, 2005, pages 19-41.

Haughey, Duncan. "A Brief History of SMART Goals." https://www.projectsmart.co.uk/brief-history-of-smart-goals.php Posted at www.projectsmart.co.uk, December 13, 2014.

Hayden, Gene C. *The Follow-Through Factor: Getting from Doubt to Done.* Toronto, CA: McClelland and Stewart, 2009

Hurtado, Maria Elena. "Only three out of ten university students graduate." April 24, 2015. University World News. Posted http://www.universityworldnews.com/article.php?story=201504219123029167

John, Arit. July 9, 2013, "The Books People Leave Unfinished" in *The Atlantic*, online version, Posted at https://www.theatlantic.

com/entertainment/archive/2013/07/most-disappointing-books-recent-publishing-history/313505/

Khadaroo, Stacy Teicher "How to get high school dropouts into 'recovery'? Ideas bloom across US.," *Christian Science Monitor*, January 15, 2013, posted at https://www.csmonitor.com/USA/2013/0115/How-to-get-high-school-dropouts-into-recovery-Ideas-bloom-across-US

Knight, Sarah. *Get Your Sh*t Together: How to Stop Worrying About What You Should Do So You Can Finish What You Need to Do and Start Doing What You Want to Do (A No F*cks Given Guide)*. NY: Little, Brown, 2016.

Kondo, Marie. *The Life-Changing Magic of Tidying Up.* New York: Ten Speed Press, 2014.

Lakein, Alan. *How to Get Control of Your Time and Your Life.* Signet, 1989 (1973).

Levinson, Steven and Peter Greider. *Following Through: A Revolutionary New Model for Finishing Whatever You Start.* Third edition. (Createspace, 2015; 1st edition, Kensington Publishing, 1998).

______________ and Chris Cooper. *The Power to Get Things Done: (Whether You Feel Like It or Not)* by. NY: Perigee, an imprint of Penguin Random House, 2015.

Luongo, Janet. 365 *Daily Affirmations for Creativity.* Foreword by Jack Canfield. Stamford, CT: Hannacroix Creek Books, Inc., 2005. Audiobook version, 2013. E-book version, 2016.

Luke, Ali. "How to Finish What You Start: A Five-Step Plan for Writers." June 15, 2015. Posted at WritetoDone, https://writetodone.com/how-to-finish-what-you-start-a-five-step-plan-for-writers/

Mann, Dominic. *Get Stuff* Done by Dominic Mann. 2016.

Matlen, Terry. T*he Queen of Distraction: How Women with ADD Can Conquer Chaos, Find Focus, and Get It All Done.* Oakland, CA: New Harbinger Publications, 2014.

Morgenstern, Julie. *Time Management from the Inside Out.* 2nd edition. New York: Holt, 2004.

National Institute of Mental Health (NIMH), "Attention Hyperactivity Deficit Disorder" posted at https://www.nimh.nih.gov/health/topics/attention-deficit-hyperactivity-disorder-adhd/index.shtml#part_145447 (Last revised March 2016)

Oxford English Dictionary. "deadline." Oxford University Press. 2018 (online)

Oyama, Yoshinori, Emmanuel Manalo, and Yoshihide Nakatani. "The Hemingway Effect: How failing to finish a task can have a positive effect on motivation." Science Direct, Thinking Skills and Creativity. Available February 2, 2018. Posted through Creative Commons license at https://www.sciencedirect.com/science/article/pii/S187118711730189X

Porter, Jane. "Why You Can Never Finish Anything and How to Finally Change It." Posted at Fast Company online, February 03, 2014.

Rayome, Alison DeNisco. "Distracted Minds: 3 Tips to Disconnect from Tech and Increase Productivity." November 16, 2016. Published in TechRepublic. Posted at https://www.techrepublic.com/article/distracted-minds-3-tips-to-disconnect-from-tech-and-increase-productivity/

Rizzo, Paula. *Listful Thinking: Using Lists to be More productive, Highly Successful, and Less Stressed.* Foreword by Julie Morgenstern. NY: Viva Editions, 2014.

Sandberg, Jared. "Rise of False Deadline Means Truly Urgent Often Gets Done Late." *Wall Street Journal,* January 23, 2007.

Schuman, Rebecca. "ABD Company." Posted on Slate http://www.

slate.com/articles/life/education/2014/08/abds all but dissertation phd candidates who cant quite finish.html August 1, 2014.

Stack, Laura. *Doing the Right Things Right.* Oakland, CA: Berrett Koehler Publishers, 2016.

SWNS. "Americans check their phones 80 times a day: study." Posted on November 8, 2017. https://nypost.com/2017/11/08/americans-check-their-phones-80-times-a-day-study/

Waldron, Travis. "Nearly Half of All America's College Students Drop Out Before Receiving a Degree," March 28, 2012, Think Progress, Posted at https://thinkprogress.org/study-nearly-half-of-americas-college-students-drop-out-before-receiving-a-degree-68867634fa5e/

Waters, Kelly. "Stop Starting, Start Finishing. Unfinished Work is Debt." All About Agile, posted at http://www.allaboutagile.com, June 15,2015.

"What Does SMART Mean?" posted at Mindtools.com https://www.mindtools.com/pages/article/smart-goals.htm

Wheelis, Allen. *How People Change.* NY: Harper & Row, 1973.

Winter, Arthur and Ruth Winter. *Brain Workout*. NY: St. Martin's Press, 1997.

Yager, Jan. *125 Ways to Meet the Love of Your Life* (Second edition). Stamford, CT: Hannacroix Creek Books, Inc., 2016, 2004.

__________. *365 Daily Affirmations for Time Management.* Stamford, CT: Hannacroix Creek Books, 2011.

__________. *Creative Time Management for the New Millennium* Stamford, CT: Hannacroix Creek Books, 1999.

__________. *Delivering Time Management for IT Professionals: A Trainer's Manual.* Birmingham, UK: Packt, 2015.

_________. "Permanent Delegation." *EXEC* magazine. Spring 1995, pages 78-81.

_________. *Productive Relationships: 57 Strategies for Building Stronger Business Connections.* Stamford, CT: Hannacroix Creek Books, Inc., 2011.

_________. *Work Less, Do More: The 7-Day Productivity Makeover* (Third edition). Stamford, CT: Hannacroix Creek Books, Inc., 2017, 2012; 1st edition, 2008, Sterling Publishing, Inc.

_________. *The Fast Track Guide to Losing Weight and Keeping It Off* Stamford, CT: Hannacroix Creek Books, Inc., 2015.

_________. *Put More Time on Your Side* (2nd edition) Shippensburg, PA: Sound Wisdom, 2017.

Resources*

Associations, online goal-setting, to-do list, and time management, and related programs

*Inclusion in this list does not imply an endorsement nor does omission indicate anything negative about products or websites that are missing. This listing is for information purposes only. Furthermore, websites may change or even disappear from the Internet. Evaluate each listing on your own.

Related associations or companies

Project Management Institute (PMI)

http://pmi.org

Headquartered near Philadelphia, this is the education and certification organization for project managers.

NAPO® (National Association of Productivity & Organizing Professionals)™

http://napo.net

An association of more than 3,500 organizing professionals. Maintains a directory of members that you can search if you are looking for someone to work with. There is an annual education conference for members.

Attention Deficit Disorder Association (ADDA)

https://add.org

Volunteer, international, virtual-run organization without a physical office.

ADD Consults

www.ADDConsults.com

Provides a directory as well as resources on ADD for women. Started and run by Terry Matlen, a clinical social worker with ADHD who has written and spoken extensively on this issue.

CHADD- The National Resource on ADHD

http://www.chadd.org/

4601 Presidents Drive, Suite 300

Lanham, MD 20706

A membership organization for those with ADHD as well as their parents and caregivers and educators. Organizes a national annual conference on ADHD.

Membership organization with support groups, training, and events.

www.timeman.com

Site for the National Management Institution (NMI) and for Peter Turla, former NASA rocket designer who conducts time management training. This Dallas, Texas-based time management training center has a team of trainers as well as two self-paced courses that could be bought for online delivery.

www.drjanyager.com

My website where you'll find a link to several of my time management books as well as published articles or blogs on time management. At the site, you can sign up for the free mailing which will enable you to keep up with my latest publications, special offers, as well as upcoming seminars or author events or appearances.

Productivity apps/websites/companies

Wunderlist

https://www.wunderlist.com/

This is an app that enables you to bring your to-do lists with you, syncing it with your tablet, computer, or smartphone.

Evernote

https://evernote.com

Free app for writing everything down and keeping track of your goals. There is also a business version for $12.50/month, billed annually.

Paper

http://www.fiftythree.com

Developed by FiftyThree, Inc.

Available through iTunes, this app enables you to make lists, draw, and do related tasks. Paper is free for iPhone and the iPad.

OneNote

https://www.onenote.com

Developed by Microsoft and available for free to put notes and to-do lists on your computer, phone, or table.

Dropbox

www.dropbox.com

Convenient way to store key documents that you can access from anywhere. Has a free version but there is a cap on how much storage you can get. After that, there are various payment plans for more storage space.

Calendar apps

There are so many available calendar apps, I think it best to provide you with the url for the comprehensive article reviewing 20+ options, including a couple that are free, written by John Corpuz for Toms Guide: https://www.tomsguide.com/us/pictures-story/442-best-calendar-apps.html

At-a Glance®

www.ataglance.com

ACCO Brands Direct

P.O. Box 400

Sidney, NY 13838-0400

Manufacturers of various appointment calendars that enable you to track your day in fifteen minute increments (my personal favorite, Product Number G520H, DayMinder® Weekly Appointment Book, the hardcover version), weekly or monthly. Available through direct order from the website or at your favorite online or local office supply store.

Goal-setting programs

https://www.stickk.com/

Based on the concept of a Commitment Contract, this program was co-founded by Yale University professors including Economic Professor Dean Karlan. Other co-founders are Jordan Goldberg and Ian Ayres and Victoria Fenar. Although the examples at the site are based on quite hefty financial incentives, you could certainly use the concept with less costly rewards.

http://weekplan.net/

Inspired by Covey's *The 7 Habits of Highly Effective People* and

Allen's *Getting Things Done*, developed by Aymeric Gaurat-Apelli. Has a free 7-day trial and two plans that cost 0.83 and $1 weekly billed annually.

http://lifetick.com/

Fee-based service ($14/month) developed by an Australian company in 2008, Meridian 86, that is also based on the SMART criteria for goal-setting. There is also a 30 day free trial.

Miscellaneous websites you might find useful

https://www.lumosity.com

Site that offers building concentration activities. Offers a free account that enables you to try three brain exercises.

www.LinkedIn.com

Storing your business connections through this global database with more than 500 million users. Ideally you will already have some sort of connection to those you are linked to but, a lot of business people connect to those that are unknown to them but with whom they would like to develop a connection.

www.Timeanddate.com

Free cite that enables you to figure out what time it is anywhere in the world at that moment in case you want to make a phone call to someone or send a text message and you would prefer that it not arrive in the middle of the night!

www.xe.com

Free and quick wave to find out how much a currency is worth in another currency. Just put the amount of money you want to convert, in the current currency, and then put in the currency you want to convert to, click on the conversion "button," and you'll have your answer instantly.

www.Twitter.com

This free site offers you a chance to growing your platform or build a brand for yourself, your product, or your company. You can also try to connect to movers and shakers by following, and commenting on, their tweets.

HotelTonight
https://www.hoteltonight.com/
An app for getting a last-minute booking at a hotel.

GrubHub
https://www.grubhub.com/
An app for ordering online and getting immediate delivery.

Conducting research
https://surveymonkey.com
Enables subscribes to electronically send out surveys to selective respondents or, through their Audience response paid service, to anonymous paid respondents from throughout the United States and internationally. There is a free version of surveymonkey that allows you to send out a survey with up to 10 questions on your own.

Google
https://www.google.com/forms/about/
Search engine Google has a version with surveys and forms that enables you to conduct research for free.

APPENDIX

How I Went About Researching This Book

How to Finish Everything You Start draws on my sociology and psychology graduate training, all the research I have conducted, as well as my teaching experiences, at colleges and coaching or facilitating time management workshops at companies, agencies, associations, or with individuals. I have even taught a four-week College for Kids course in time management to fourth graders!

In addition to reviewing the hundreds of surveys or interviews conducted for previous books looking for responses related to finishing that might be helpful in this new work, I collected additional research focused on finishing. That new research included analyzing the results of a 10-question survey completed by 205 anonymous men and women distributed through surveymonkey.com's Audience Response program which allows you to purchase anonymous respondents. I also invited additional men and women to answer an expanded version of that finishing survey by placing a query in HELP (Help a Reporter Out). Thirty-eight (38) men and women answered an expanded version of my survey which enabled me to do selected follow-up by e-mail or phone. The 243 respondents for both these surveys focusing on finishing were from throughout the United States as well as from India, China, Latvia, Australia, Germany, New Zealand, Vietnam, Canada, South Africa, the United Kingdom, and other countries.

Finally, I consulted books and articles related to this issue, as noted in the "Selected Bibliography Including Cited Works" and highlighted at the end of this book in the more focused list that I created entitled for those who want to offer training on *How to Finish Everything You Start*, "Selected Books on Finishing" for use in Workshops or In-House Training.

ACTION! STRATEGY WORKSHEET*

(A more detailed discussion of the ACTION! System is in Chapter 7, "Taking Control: Goal Setting and Prioritizing")

Project or Task: ______________________________

A (Assess): ______________________________

____

____

C (Control): ______________________________

____

____

T (Target): ______________________________

____

____

I (Innovate): ______________________________

____

____

O (Organized): ______________________________

____

____

N! (Now!): ______________________________

____

____

ACTION! STRATEGY WORKSHEET*

(A more detailed discussion of the ACTION! System is in Chapter 7, "Taking Control: Goal Setting and Prioritizing")

Project or Task: ______________________________

A (Assess): ______________________________

____

____

C (Control): ______________________________

____

____

T (Target): ______________________________

____

____

I (Innovate): ______________________________

____

____

O (Organized): ______________________________

____

____

N! (Now!): ______________________________

____

____

MY TO-DO LIST

Today's Date ________

	To Do	**Time to Complete**	**Completed (Date)**
Project ________ (or tasks within one project)			
#1			
#2			
#3			
#4			
#5			
#6			
Chores (or errands)			
#1			
#2			
#3			
#4			
#5			
#6			

MY TO-DO LIST

Today's date ___________

	To do	Time to complete	Completed (date)
Project	________________________		
(Tasks within one project)			
#1			
#2			
#3			
#4			
#5			
#6			
#7			
#8			
#9			
#10			
#11			
#12			
Chores (or errands)			
#1			
#2			
#3			
#4			
#5			
#6			

The 7 Principles of Creative Time Management*

*Slightly edited and reprinted, with permission, from *Creative Time Management for the New Millennium* by Jan Yager, Ph.D. (Hannacroix Creek Books, Inc., 1999, pages 10-13.)

1. Be Active, Not Reactive.

   Make active decision about how you spend your time instead of reacting to every demand on you.

2. Set Goals.

   Setting long- and short-term goals help you know where you are going and what you have to do to get there. It will help you to track what tasks or projects that are unfinished that you need to complete.

3. Prioritize actions.

   After your goals are stable, prioritize what you do to achieve each one. Be careful not to let tasks, projects, or relationships that you value fall between the cracks and stay undone.

4. Keep your focus.

   Concentrate on one major project at a time even if you jump around on how you complete that project. Whatever the task is that you commit to for all the right reasons, give it your all and keep going till you finish it.

5. Create realistic deadlines.

   Deadlines, particularly realistic ones, will assist you in keeping your focus on specific long-term goals and especially on short-term priorities. A deadline that is too far into the future will make it harder to avoid getting committed to too many competing tasks or projects. A deadline that is too soon opens the likelihood that you will be frustrated that you are either working at a pace that is hard to maintain or that you will have to ask for one or more extensions. Try to learn how long tasks really take so you create a realistic deadline, adding just enough time to give yourself an extra cushion in line with the maxim, "Promise less, deliver more."

6. D-O I-T N-O-W – Applying this acronym on a regular basis will help you to maximize your productivity:

D = Divide and conquer what you must do.

O = Organize your materials, how you will do it.

I = Ignore interruptions that are annoying distractions.

T = Take the time to learn how to do things yourself.

N – Now, not tomorrow. Don't procrastinate.

O = Opportunity is knocking. Take advantage of opportunities.

W = Watch out for time gobblers. Keep track of, and in control of, how much time you spend on the Internet, on social media, reading and sending E-mails, watching TV, talking on the phone, or sending, and receiving, text messages.

7. Balance your life.

   This 7th principle may be the most important one of all. By making the time for those you care about —your romantic partner (spouse), children—young and grown—grandchildren, siblings, extended family, friends, neighbors, volunteer groups, colleagues, and even pets—your work will be key in your life but not your entire life as you have the fuller life that we all deserve. Part of balancing your life is also to make time for yourself whether that means making the time to exercise, reading books for pleasure, taking in cultural, sports, or music events just for fun, and whatever else you care about that needs to be part of your life and can be when you practice creative time management.

DAILY TIME LOG 1

TODAY'S DATE: ________________

DAY OF THE WEEK: __________

TYPE OF DAY: ________________ (Work? School? Leisure?)

TIME	ACTIVITY
______	*Wake Up*
______	________________________________
______	________________________________
______	________________________________
______	________________________________
______	________________________________
______	________________________________
______	________________________________
______	________________________________
______	________________________________
______	________________________________
______	________________________________
______	________________________________
______	________________________________
______	________________________________
______	________________________________

Conclude your day with the time you go to sleep:

______	________________________________

COMMENTS (Try to notice if there are any times when you are especially alert, or particularly tired, as well as any peaks of efficiency, periods of heightened concentration, and times when you pay better attention to details. At what times are you better or worse at working with people—both in person and over the phone?)

____

____

____

____

____

DAILY TIME LOG 2

TODAY'S DATE: ________________

DAY OF THE WEEK: ___________

TYPE OF DAY: ________________ (Work? School? Leisure?)

TIME	ACTIVITY
______	*Wake Up*
______	______________________________
______	______________________________
______	______________________________
______	______________________________
______	______________________________
______	______________________________
______	______________________________
______	______________________________
______	______________________________
______	______________________________
______	______________________________
______	______________________________
______	______________________________

_______ ______________________________

_______ ______________________________

Conclude your day with the time you go to sleep:

_______ ______________________________

COMMENTS (Try to notice if there are any times when you are especially alert, or particularly tired, as well as any peaks of efficiency, periods of heightened concentration, and times when you pay better attention to details. At what times are you better or worse at working with people—both in person and over the phone?)

____

____

____

____

____

Appointment Planner

Day __________ **Date** __________

12:00 A.M. ______________________

1:00 ____________________________

2:00 ____________________________

3:00 ____________________________

4:00 ____________________________

4:15 ____________________________

4:30 ____________________________

4:45 ____________________________

5:00 ____________________________

5:15 ____________________________

5:30 ____________________________

5:45 ____________________________

6:00 ____________________________

6:15 ____________________________

6:30 ____________________________

6:45 ____________________________

7:00 ____________________________

7:15 ______________________________

7:30 ______________________________

7:45 ______________________________

8:00 ______________________________

8:15 ______________________________

8:30 ______________________________

8:45 ______________________________

9:00 ______________________________

9:15 ______________________________

9:30 ______________________________

9:45 ______________________________

10:00 ____________________________

10:15 ____________________________

10:30 ____________________________

10:45 ____________________________

11:00 ____________________________

11:15 ____________________________

11:30 ____________________________

11:45 ____________________________

12:00 P.M. ________________________

12:15 ______________________________

12:30 ______________________________

12:45 ______________________________

1:00 ______________________________

1:15 ______________________________

1:30 ______________________________

1:45 ______________________________

2:00 ______________________________

2:15 ______________________________

2:30 ______________________________

2:45 ______________________________

3:00 ______________________________

3:15 ______________________________

3:30 ______________________________

3:45 ______________________________

4:00 ______________________________

4:15 ______________________________

4:30 ______________________________

4:45 ______________________________

5:00 ______________________________

5:15 ______________________________

5:30 ______________________________

5:45 ______________________________

6:00 ______________________________

6:15 ______________________________

6:30 ______________________________

6:45 ______________________________

7:00 ______________________________

7:15 ______________________________

7:30 ______________________________

7:45 ______________________________

8:00 ______________________________

8:30 ______________________________

9:00 ______________________________

9:30 ______________________________

10:00 ____________________________

10:30 ____________________________

11:00 ____________________________

11:30 ____________________________

12:00 A.M. _______________________

Selected Books on Finishing

Acuff, Jon. *Finish: Give Yourself the Gift of Done* by Jon Acuff. New York: Portfolio (Penguin Random House Company), 2017.

Covey, Stephen. *7 Habits of Highly Effective People: Powerful Lessons in Personal Change.* NY: Simon & Schuster/Fireside, 1989.

Hayden, Gene C. *The Follow-Through Factor: Getting from Doubt to Done.* Toronto, CA: McClelland and Stewart, 2009

Levinson, Steve and Peter Greider. *Following Through: A Revolutionary New Model for Finishing Whatever You Start.* Third edition. (Createspace, 2015; 1st edition, Kensington Publishing, 1998).

Levinson, Steve and Chris Cooper. *The Power to Get Things Done: (Whether You Feel Like It or Not)* by. NY: Perigee, an imprint of Penguin Random House, 2015.

Yager, Jan. *How to Finish Everything You Start.* Stamford, CT: Hannacroix Creek Books, Inc., 2019. Available at online and local booksellers. For bulk orders, contact the publisher directly: hannacroix@aol.com. In the subcontinent of India, published by Jaico Publishing, Mumbai, 2019.

Reading Group or Discussion Guide
for How to Finish Everything You Start
By Jan Yager, Ph.D.

Discussion Points:

1. In Chapter 2, "The Reasons Are Within You," Dr. Yager lists 22 possible reasons you may have a finishing challenge in general or on a project or task. Consider something you currently have unfinished that is bothering you. Review the 22 potential reasons in Chapter 2 and write down one or more of those reasons that might help you to get this project or venture done.

   Unfinished project, task, or venture: ______________

   Top reasons from Chapter 2 that it's unfinished:

   1. ____
   2. ____
   3. ____

2. One of the themes to *How to Finish Everything You Start* is that you need to be selective about what you finish, as well as the order in which you complete things. Is that your attitude toward finishing or do you have a different view? Discuss the criteria you apply to finishing that might help you to get more of the important things done.
3. Do you find a "to-do" list helpful? If you do, what kind are you currently using? Pen or pencil and paper? Electronic version? A list-making app? (There are many included in the Resource section if you want to try a new one.) How can you start using a "to-do" list more effectively, if you are not doing that currently? If you do use a "to-do" list, how can you make yours more

effective helping you to finish more of what you need to — want to — do.

4. Review Chapter 10, "Becoming a Better Delegator." What is your number one "take away" from that chapter that will help you with delegating?

    ____

    ____

5. How can Dr. Yager's suggestions in Chapter 9, "Learning to Say 'No,'' help you to get more done?
6. Chapter 11 applies Dr. Yager's F-I-N-I-S-H acronym to the major task of writing —and finishing —a book. Now select a complex task that you must do for work or in your personal life and apply the F-I-N-I-S-H acronym to that task. (If necessary, refer to Chapter 6, "Using F-I-N-I-S-H.)
7. Do you formalize your short- and long-term goals? If "yes," write down your key personal and professional goals for the next hour, day, week, year, and 5 years. If "no," do you want to start formalizing your goals? What ideas in Chapter 7, "Taking Control: Goal Setting and Prioritizing," will help you to set goals?
8. When, if ever, is it time to leave a project unfinished or to abandon a venture? Consider some of the perspectives on this that Dr. Yager shares in Chapter 12.
9. What might you do if someone on your team has a finishing problem? (Consider some of the suggestions in Chapter 13, "Concluding Thoughts," in the section entitled, "When You Are Not the Problem."
10. Rewards are a great motivator for finishing for yourself or for your department or company. Do you have rewards in place yet? If not, what are some ways you might use financial rewards, such as a bonus, or

motivational rewards, like praise or even awards, to reinforce the benefits of finishing?

11. How can the concept of The Hemingway Effect —the insight that having something closer to finishing helps to finish it more than if there is more to do —help you with your finishing challenges?
12. Do you find yourself doing too much at once? If you do, what are the ways that you can discipline yourself, or change your work environment, so you can focus more on priorities, completing things till it is finished, before moving on to the next priority? Would the idea of selective attention that Dr. Yager explores in this book help you or do you know yourself well enough to know that you must adhere to a strict "one thing at a time till finished" approach?
13. What is the idea in *How to Finish Everything You Start* that you most disagree with and why? What is your alternative view or approach?
14. What is the concept in *How to Finish Everything You Start* that resonates the most with you and why? How will that concept be most helpful to you, so you can finish what you start?
15. Do you have a Wish List of "big" things you want to finish over your lifetime? Some you might not even have started yet! Make that list now so you have a concrete reminder of what you want to accomplish.

A Note to Readers or Workshop Participants:

One of the advantages of writing a follow-up book to a topic that I have been researching for so many decades is that I am able to observe how the issue has changed over the years. Yes, there are concepts that I was researching and writing about, and conducting workshops on, back in the 1980s that are still viable today, like creating a "to-do" list, learning to say "no," dealing with procrastination and perfectionism, and having too much to do.

But, over time, I have seen that some of those issues have gotten even more problematic and the nature of how a concept is dealt with, like a "to do" list, may have gone from writing it down on paper to using a website or an app. But the premise is still the same: keeping track of what you must do.

I noticed that finishing things has become a bigger problem than ever before. It's not just the big things, like books that are half-written or abandoned after one or two chapters, or college or graduate degrees that are set aside even after years of effort, expense, energy, and time, as well as even relationships that are ended too soon when it could have been salvaged.

How to Finish Everything You Start has been an amazing journey for me to research and write since it has drawn on my previous knowledge from the six other time management books I've published but it also is based on the insights from 243 surveys and/or follow-up interviews focusing on the finishing issue.

Yes, writing an entire book on one key challenge, finishing, has proven to be a much different experience than I anticipated when I first conceived of the book many months ago. I soon realized that to conquer that one issue — finishing — would draw on everything I have learned about time management, productivity, relationships, and human nature over the years, and then some.

Discussing the issues related to finishing with a reading group or in a workshop setting may be a useful way to explore the themes and ideas you have explored in this book, expanding the examples and anecdotes from my own experiences, as well as from the survey respondents or interviewees, with your own occurrences as well as those of your friends, colleagues, reading, or discussion group members. As you share, remember one of the rules of brainstorming: there is no right or wrong idea; everyone can share in a safe and open atmosphere even if you disagree with someone's perspective.

About Dr. Jan Yager

Besides *How to Finish Everything You Start*, Dr. Yager's time management books include *Creative Time Management for the New Millennium; Put More Time on Your Side; Work Less, Do More: The 7-Day Productivity Makeover; Delivering Time Management to IT Professionals: A Training Manual* and *365 Daily Affirmations for Time Management.* For more on Dr. Yager, or to contact her about coaching, conducting a workshop, or a writing project, e-mail her at jyager@aol.com, go to www.drjanyager.com, or to her profile on www.Linkedin.com/in/drjanyager

About the Author

Dr. Jan Yager, who holds a Ph.D. in sociology from The City University of New York Graduate Center, a master's in criminal justice, and did graduate work in art therapy, has been conducting time management workshops throughout the U.S. and internationally since 1984, when her first book on time management, *Creative Time Management,* was published.

A prolific writer, Dr. Yager is the award-winning author of 46 books, translated into 33 languages, including six on time management —*Creative Time Management for the New Millennium; 365 Daily Affirmations for Time Management; Delivering Time Management to IT Professionals: A Trainer's Manual; Put More Time on Your Side; Work Less, Do More: The 7-Day Productivity Makeover;* and *Creative Time Management;* and two books that apply time management to life's issues — *125 Ways to Meet the Love of Your Life* and *The Fast Track Guide to Losing Weight and Keeping It Off.* Her books on other topics include — *When Friendship Hurts; Friendshifts; 365 Daily Affirmations on Healthy & Nurturing Relationships; Productive Relationships; Career Opportunities in the Publishing Industry; Career Opportunities in the Film Industry* among other titles.

Dr. Yager's time management workshops, and keynote addresses, have been offered throughout the United States and internationally including in India.

To reach Jan for speaking engagements, contact your favorite lecture bureau. For coaching, consulting, or writing projects, contact the author directly at jyager@aol.com. For more information, visit http://www.drjanyager.com.

Other time management books by Dr. Jan Yager published by Jaico Publishing that may be of interest

Work Less, Do More

The 7-Day Productivity Makeover

2017

254 pages

On the heels of her popular 14-day version published a decade ago, Dr. Yager has revised and updated her program so you can accomplish it in just seven days without missing out on any key concepts. This is in recognition of how much more time-strapped everyone is today with the drive to accomplish as much as possible – as quickly as you can and without sacrificing quality – stronger than ever.

Here is what's covered:

Day 1/ Getting Started and Goal Setting

Day 2/ Dealing With the 5-Ps: Procrastination; Perfectionism; Poor Planning; Poor Pacing; and Petulance – and 8 More Time Blocks

Day 3/ Prioritizing, Multitasking, and Delegating

Day 4/ Getting Organized and Mastering Paperwork

Day 5/ More Effective Ways to Use the Phone, Other Equipment, and E-Mail

Day 6/ Handling Change, Interruptions or Distractions, and Deadlines

Day 7/ Improving Relationships, Balancing Your Life, and Teaching Time Management to Children and Teens

Well-written, and filled with anecdotes, examples, self-quizzes and worksheets, Dr. Yager also shares the results of her original time management surveys of more than 250 men and women on their time challenges, strengths, and preferred productivity tools.

JAICO PUBLISHING HOUSE

Elevate Your Life. Transform Your World.

ESTABLISHED IN 1946, Jaico Publishing House is home to world-transforming authors such as Sri Sri Paramahansa Yogananda, Osho, the Dalai Lama, Sri Sri Ravi Shankar, Sadhguru, Robin Sharma, Deepak Chopra, Jack Canfield, Eknath Easwaran, Devdutt Pattanaik, Khushwant Singh, John Maxwell, Brian Tracy, and Stephen Hawking.

Our late founder Mr. Jaman Shah first established Jaico as a book distribution company. Sensing that independence was around the corner, he aptly named his company Jaico ('Jai' means victory in Hindi). In order to service the significant demand for affordable books in a developing nation, Mr. Shah initiated Jaico's own publications. Jaico was India's first publisher of paperback books in the English language.

While self-help, religion and philosophy, mind/body/spirit, and business titles form the cornerstone of our non-fiction list, we publish an exciting range of travel, current affairs, biography, and popular science books as well. Our renewed focus on popular fiction is evident in our new titles by a host of fresh young talent from India and abroad. Jaico's recently established translations division translates selected English content into nine regional languages.

Jaico distributes its own titles. With its headquarters in Mumbai, Jaico has branches in Ahmedabad, Bangalore, Chennai, Delhi, Hyderabad, and Kolkata.

SINCE 1946